THE COMPLETE CASES OF JOHN SMITH,
VOLUME 1

OTHER BOOKS IN THE DIME DETECTIVE UNIFORM EDITION LIBRARY:

The Complete Cases of the Acme Indemnity Op by Jan Dana

The Complete Cases of Bill Brent by Frederick C. Davis

The Complete Cases of Mike Blair by Hank Searls

The Complete Cases of Uncle Tubby by Ray Cummings

The Complete Cases of Val Easton by T.T. Flynn

THE COMPLETE CASES OF

VOLUME 1

WYATT BLASSINGAME

ILLUSTRATIONS BY
AMOS SEWELL

STEEGER BOOKS • 2020

© 2020 Steeger Properties, LLC • First Edition—2020

PUBLISHING HISTORY

"He Kills in Darkness" originally appeared in the June 1937 issue of *Detective Tales* magazine. Copyright 1937 by Popular Publications, Inc. Copyright renewed 1964 and assigned to Steeger Properties, LLC. All rights reserved.

"No Parole for the Dead" originally appeared in the July 1937 issue of *Detective Tales* magazine. Copyright 1937 by Popular Publications, Inc. Copyright renewed 1964 and assigned to Steeger Properties, LLC. All rights reserved.

"No Parole from Hell" originally appeared in the August 1937 issue of *Detective Tales* magazine. Copyright 1937 by Popular Publications, Inc. Copyright renewed 1964 and assigned to Steeger Properties, LLC. All rights reserved.

"Death Breaks Parole" originally appeared in the December 1937 issue of *Detective Tales* magazine. Copyright 1937 by Popular Publications, Inc. Copyright renewed 1964 and assigned to Steeger Properties, LLC. All rights reserved.

"Death Trap for the Parole Killer" originally appeared in the May 1938 issue of *Detective Tales* magazine. Copyright 1938 by Popular Publications, Inc. Copyright renewed 1965 and assigned to Steeger Properties, LLC. All rights reserved.

"Murder Gives No Parole" originally appeared in the June 1938 issue of *Detective Tales* magazine. Copyright 1938 by Popular Publications, Inc. Copyright renewed 1965 and assigned to Steeger Properties, LLC. All rights reserved.

ALL RIGHTS RESERVED

No part of this book may be reproduced or utilized in any form or by any means, electronic or mechanical, without permission in writing from the publisher.

This edition has been marked via subtle changes, so anyone who reprints from this collection is committing a violation of copyright.

"John Smith" and "Dime Detective" are trademarks of Steeger Properties, LLC.

TABLE OF CONTENTS

HE KILLS IN DARKNESS 1

NO PAROLE FOR THE DEAD 27

NO PAROLE FROM HELL 65

DEATH BREAKS PAROLE 105

DEATH TRAP FOR THE PAROLE KILLER. . . . 141

MURDER GIVES NO PAROLE 197

HE KILLS IN DARKNESS

PEOPLE THOUGHT SMITH A STRANGE MAN—BUT THEY NEVER DREAMED HOW EFFICIENTLY DEADLY HE MIGHT BE. ONE MAN FOUND OUT—WHEN SMITH CAME BACK FROM HELL TO EXACT FROM HIM A WEIRD AND TERRIFYING JUSTICE....

T HE NURSE came quietly into the room, rubber heels silent on the hard rubber flooring. Just over the sill she paused, holding the knob of the still-open door.

A man was sitting in a chair near the window on the far side of the room. There was a heavy bandage over his eyes. Without turning he said, "Come on in, Nurse. The doctor will be here soon, won't he?"

"Well I'll declare, Mr. Smith," she said, closing the door behind her, "you certainly have remarkable ears. I didn't make any noise at all. How'd you know it was me?"

"I heard you coming down the hallway," he said. "I recognized your step. When a man's blind he learns to use his other senses. Everybody could have better ears if they trained them. And noses too. I can just about smell my way around."

"You certainly can," the nurse said. "I've seen you almost run into a wall and then stop, like you could tell it was there. And you can find almost anything in this room too."

"But I can't see," the man said. His voice was suddenly harsh and tight with emotion. "For ten years I haven't been able to see. Ten years in solid darkness. Try shutting your eyes and think: 'I can't open them. I'll never be able to open them, never be able to see again!' Try to realize what it means to be blind!"

"Now don't get excited, Mr. Smith," the nurse said. "You've been such a good patient. And Dr. Thorn will be here soon."

The man put amazingly white hands on the arms of his chair and fisted them. "All right," he said. "I'll keep steady. But I want to talk. I'm really afraid, you know. I keep thinking: 'Suppose the operation wasn't effective? Suppose the doctor takes off the bandage and I can't even tell it's gone? I'll be blind forever then. I won't even have hope.' But I *know* I'm going to be able to see. I've got to! I've got a job to do."

"All right," the nurse said. "Talk if it helps. I never did know just what sort of accident you had."

"**IT WASN'T** an accident," Smith said and it seemed to the nurse that despite the bandage she could see into his eyes, see them staring through an endless tunnel of darkness back to that last brilliant flash of light which had gone out ten years ago.

"I was a senior in college," he said. "I was going to graduate in another month. I had a job promised me—and a girl too. We were going to be married. Then one day on Carondelet Street I ran into the holdup of an armored truck right outside one of the banks. There were three of the crooks. They were masked. I don't think I really knew what was happening. Maybe I did; it was so quick and so long ago I can't be certain. I grabbed one of the men and he shot me. The bullet scarcely nicked my forehead, but the powder burned my eyes. I knew when I fell that I was blind. I should have been unconscious, but I wasn't. I heard the leader, the man who'd shot me, say, 'Gun that other fellow

The light blinded Smith.

who's getting in the way and let's go.' I didn't hear any more, but I remember that man's voice. Maybe it's because I already knew I was blind and was depending on my ears. I'll know that voice when I hear it again."

"And what happened to the bandits?"

"They vanished. That's why I've got to be able to see. I'm going to find those men." The paper-white hands were rigid on the chair arms. They were strong hands, the nurse thought. The whole body was strong, small but well made. Yet below the bandage the man's face was as white as his blond hair—white as if the very darkness in which he had lived so long had drained the color from his skin.

"I've got to find those men," he repeated. "That's why I've *got* to be able to see. That's why… He stopped. "The doctor's coming," he said.

The nurse listened. "I can't hear anything," she said.

"I can tell his step," Smith said. "He's half way down the hall. He'll be here in a moment." He raised one stiff hand to touch at the bandage across his eyes.

DETECTIVE LIEUTENANT Paul Rutgers didn't look the way Smith had imagined him. In the days immediately following the holdup Rutgers had called on Smith out of sympathy, reporting how the pursuit of the bandits was progressing, encouraging the young man in his fight against darkness. Smith had pictured him as a broad shouldered, square jawed, gray haired man. Instead he was small and weazened and dark. His eyes were coal-black.

Smith looked at him as only a man who has been blind for years can look. His own eyes were round and blue and slightly incredulous at the very fact of being able to see again. He noticed every wrinkle in the detective's face: the deepcut ones that curved upward from the corners of the mouth to just above the wide nostrils, the smaller ones crowfooted out from the eyes. He noted the way a beam of light came through the window to the left and all the motes that swirled in it, the dust on the floor, the empty straight chair with the wobbly left front leg. His eyes seemed to strain in an effort to see everything possible now to make up for the years of darkness.

"I've your request for a license as a private detective," Lieut. Rutgers said. "The commissioner had left the final decision up to me."

"You know why I want it," Smith said.

Rutgers tapped his desk with a blunt forefinger. "Yes." The black eyes looked at Smith for a moment, then down at the desk. "It's ten years since that holdup," he said. "The police did everything humanly possible at that time, and failed. The serial numbers on only a small amount of the money were known and those turned up, scattered about, years ago. I don't see how you can possibly hope to do anything."

"I want to try," Smith said doggedly. "There's always a chance."

Lieut. Rutgers nodded. "Maybe. We never got but one possible clue and there was no way to be certain it touched this case. About a month after the robbery a stool pigeon told us that Jackie Corsetti had turned down a job because he was already in the money. We looked up Jackie and found him—murdered. If Corsetti was tied in with that robbery, then he was the only underworld character who was. We've got a lot of stoolies around this town, but not one of them ever turned up anything."

"Listen," Smith said slowly. "When a man commits a crime like that, and gets away with it, sooner or later he's going to commit another. I want to be on hand when he does. For ten years I've been sitting in the dark—try it sometime, ten years without knowing if you'll ever see again—listening to that man's voice inside my brain. Somewhere I'll hear that voice again. And I'll recognize it."

Rutgers watched his dirty finger tap three slow beats on the desk. He looked up. "I've been thinking about that. You'll hear him and maybe know who he is—and you won't be able to prove anything. It'll take a lot more than just you saying you recognize his voice to convict him. And when you see him going free...." He looked down at his finger again.

"You mean you're afraid I'd murder him?"

"Yes."

"If I promise to keep inside the law, will I get the license?"

"You've got no experience," Rutgers said. "You can't even shoot. You won't stand a chance."

"I'm willing to risk it," Smith said. "And I can shoot. Not very well at a target I see because I haven't had any practice. But for ten years I've practiced shooting at sounds. I've been waiting for the chance to hunt the man who shot me, the other two with him."

"And you'll keep inside the law?"

"Yes."

"Then you'll get the license."

Rutgers stood up, holding out a dirty, wrinkled hand. "It's a ten year old trail," he said. "There's not much hope."

"He got away with one crime," Smith said. "When he needs money he'll try again. Sooner or later I'll find him. He'll know where his two assistants are."

THE BLACK type inserted in the personal columns of all New Orleans papers day after day read:

> Personal matters personally and discreetly handled. If you have—shall we say "difficulties"?—that you wish to be free of, refer them to John Smith, the John Smith Agency, 310 Royal Street.

"He may have something he wants done," Smith thought, "and I hope the ad will hint that I'm the sort of person he wants to do it. There's little chance he'll even remember that somebody was blinded in his holdup, still less that it was a man named John Smith. The name's so common he'll think it's faked."

But Smith didn't sit passively in his office and wait. He turned to the one place that events of ten years ago were as fresh as the day after they happened: the newspaper files. For three days he read carefully all that had happened during the month before the holdup and the two months following, and as he read he jotted down a list of names.

For two weeks he worked down that list and learned nothing. And then, with the unreal suddenness of actuality, things began to happen. He was investigating the thirty-fourth name after thirty-three failures. There was no reason to believe that this one would be different from the others.

James Brandon, a well known business man, had died of heart failure some two weeks after the holdup in which Smith had been blinded. Dr. Carter had been the attending physician and Smith called at Dr. Carter's old office address. No one there could remember him, but in an ancient city directory Smith found the doctor's home address and investigated.

It was an apartment house on Prytannia. "Dr. Carter?" the janitor asked. "Yeah, there used to be a fellow here by that name, years ago. Must be ten or more. I think he moved to Chicago, but I ain't certain. May of been some other place. Seems to me like I heard sometime after, that he died or got killed or something happened to him. I don't remember much about it."

"Thanks," Smith said. A vibrant excitement had taken hold of him. His thin nostrils flared slightly with his breathing; a faint spot of color came in his white cheeks. Perhaps this lead would fizzle out like everything else. He was just shooting in the dark anyway. "But it's a chance," he thought. "It's a chance."

HE SENT off a number of telegrams, then went back to his office. Bushelmouth Johnson, the Negro ex-prize-fighter who acted as valet and assistant for Smith, was sleeping in the cubbyhole outer office beside the telephone. Smith jabbed him in the ribs. "Quit snoring," he yelled. "Downstairs they wanted to know if I had a sawmill up here."

"Sho nuff?" Bushelmouth asked. "I ain't heard no sawmill. How come somebody put one up heauh?"

"They're planning to cut hardwood blocks out of your skull," Smith said. He went into his office and flopped down at the desk. His breath was shallow and excited as he thought back over the morning. There was just one chance in a hundred that something would pan out—but there was a chance.

The door opened to show Bushelmouth's ebon face. "Ah bet I know what dey heard," he said. "Hit was de telurphone."

Smith sat up straight. "What?"

"Us had a call," Bushelmouth said. "Ah was so s'prised hit woke me up."

"You had a relapse before I came in," Smith said. "Who was it?"

"Ah wouldn't know his name. Ah said, 'Hit's de Jawn Smiff aguncy,' and he say, 'Is Mistur Smiff dere?' and I say, 'He ain't heauh but he be heauh,' and he say 'When's dat?' and I told him 'bout 'lemen er clock. And den he say he'll call roun' den."

"It looks like business is picking up," Smith said. There was a tight smile on his face. "Maybe yet…." His voice broke off. "Somebody's coming up those stairs. A woman and she's in a hurry. Get in the other office, Bushelmouth."

"How you know dat, Mistur Smiff? Ah don't heauh nothin'."

"Get the hell in the other office! Quick!"

"Yesur." Bushelmouth's head pulled back of the door like a turtle's into its shell. The door closed.

It ripped open again a moment later and a girl came through as though flung from a catapult. She slammed the door behind her, almost smashing Bushelmouth's astonished face and feebly waving hands. Then she whirled toward Smith. "You've got to give them to me!" she cried. "You've got to! I've paid all I can. And Dave's learned who you are. He'll be here in a minute. He'll kill you!"

"What?" Smith said. His round eyes which still had the marblelike blueness of the blind stared out of his white face.

"Quick!" The girl almost choked on the word. "Dave'll kill you! I swear he will!"

SHE WOULD be pretty if her face were more composed, Smith thought. In that long period of darkness he'd forgotten how pretty a woman could be. Light reflected from the window glass touched on her hair putting a glint in its jet blackness. Her eyes were almost almond shaped, the irises a startling blue. She had been running and the exertion had whitened her face except for the splotches of rouge and lipstick.

"I'm afraid," Smith said, "there's been a mistake somewhere. I don't know who you are. I don't know what you're talking about."

"I'm Carol Duval! It's those letters you've got of mine. I've got to have them. I can't pay any more. I can't!"

"We're still on different tracks," Smith said. "Suppose you tell me who you think I am."

"I don't know," the girl cried. "But I know you've got the letters. And Dave will kill you! He's coming now...."

Smith stood up, head cocked to one side. "There's somebody coming," be said. "And in a hell of a hurry." From under his right armpit—he was left-handed—he pulled a .38 police special. "Maybe this is Dave and maybe it's not," he said. "There's a mixup somewhere. But you keep quiet and nobody'll get hurt—seriously." He stepped close to the wall where the opening floor would shelter him.

From across the room the girl watched. Her hands, whiteknuckled, were held against her open mouth. Her eyes were too wide for her face, and glassy. "Don't yell," Smith said. "Not unless you want to cause a lot of trouble."

Tn the outer office Bushelmouth said, "Well Holydamn! Folks think we givin' er barbecue de way dey...."

And a brittle voice cutting across that of the Negro. "Get the hell out of the way." The sharp crack of metal on bone. The thud of a heavy body falling in the same instant the office door slammed open. A man hurtled inside, an automatic in his right hand.

Smith said, "I'll take the gun." He had his own revolver against the man's ribs before he spoke and the newcomer realized that someone was behind him.

Smith dropped the automatic in his coat pocket. "Now," he said, "we can be calm and find out what's happening." He half turned his back and stepped toward the desk.

He heard and sensed rather than saw the movement. Even as he whirled he knew that he was too late. The man had another gun in his hand, the muzzle pointing for a spot squarely between Smith's eyes. "All right," the fellow said. "Drop that gun! Drop it or I'll blast you now!"

THE MAN was not more than twenty-three. His face was shaped like that of the girl but his eyes were black with fury. Anger had made him as insane and dangerous as a hophead. His finger twitched nervously against the halfdrawn trigger.

Smith let his revolver skid from his fingers. It was inexperience that had whipped him, he thought. He had seen the bulge in the man's pocket made by the second gun, but in his excitement he hadn't realized what it was. And he had not realized until this moment that he was afraid of death. His heart hung stiff for an endless period, then slimmed against his ribs. His face was suddenly wet with perspiration.

Somehow he kept his voice steady. "I don't know what it's all about," he said, "but let's not do anything we'll regret."

"Nobody'd regret killing a snake," the young man said. From the corner of his eye he saw the girl sidling toward him. He stepped back. "Keep out of this, Sis. I'll shoot him if you try to grab my gun. I swear to God I will."

"You must be Dave Duval," Smith said. "Your sister told me you'd be here." He was speaking loudly to cover the sounds from the outer office. "She mentioned some letters you wanted. Unfortunately…."

"You'll give them to her," Duval said, "or you'll never have any need for them. Where are they?" His finger kept twitching against the trigger. His thin, dark face was drawn with fury. His mouth worked.

"The letters aren't here," Smith said. His voice was loud enough to smother the noise of Bushelmouth coming through the door behind Duval. "I don't know who you think I am but whoever it is, I'm not." He spoke quickly, sharply. Bushelmouth was very close to Dave now and directly behind him.

And then Bushelmouth Johnson said, "Ah tried to keep him out, Mistur Smiff, but...."

Duval jumped and spun. Headlong Smith dived for him. Dave saw him, checked himself and twisted back toward the detective.

With eyes that blindness had taught to see Smith watched the scene even while he was in the air. He saw the young man's body raised on the balls of the feet, turning. He saw the sweep of elbow and wrist as the gun came round, halfing, quartering the distance. He knew that the gun would cover him before he could reach it. The shot would catch him full in the chest.

Bushelmouth Johnson struck out with the smooth-flowing punch that once had made him a topflight heavyweight. The blow landed flush on Dave Duval's jaw, lifted and slammed him across the room. He hit the wall and stood there for a moment as though nailed to it. Then his knees sagged and he went down. The girl cried out, a sort of choked sob, and ran to him.

SMITH GOT up from where his dive had carried him. His hands were trembling as he collected the guns and his heart ached. It was a full ten seconds before he turned to look at the negro. He said, "Damn you, Bushelmouth. What are you trying to do, be spectacular?"

"Who? I ain't done nothin' but get socked on de head wid dis gentleman's gun. Hit made me daisy fer a minute, then I come in heauh to see was dere some trouble maybe."

"What the hell was the idea? You were right behind him where you could have got him easily; then you had to speak and make him turn around."

"Yesur," Bushelmouth said, "Ah sho did, didn't I? But to tell you de truf, Mistur Smiff, he was such a nice lookin' young fellow Ah was scared to sock him less'n you said so. Ah knew if y'all was jus arguin' and I banged him, you'd sho get mad. Then I seen he true-for-God was gona shoot, so I let him have it."

"Okay," Smith said. "And any time you see anybody pointing a gun at me, you let 'em have it. It's a bonus of a quart of Bay St. Louis corn each time, starting with this one."

"Yesur! Ah sho do like me dat Bay St. Louis Corn. Hit ain't none like it round heauh." As he went into the outer office his long tongue snaked from corner to corner of his mouth, which was no mean journey.

Carol Duval was cradling her brother's head in her lap, but he was conscious now. He blinked, then got up, holding to the wall. "Sit down," Smith said. "Both of you be comfortable. Maybe now we can find out what it's all about."

It was blackmail. "The letters were to a married man" Carol Duval said. Her teeth dug at roughed lips, seeming to gash them with whiteness. She looked at Smith defiantly. "I love him and he loves me. His wife's been an invalid for years. She can't live much longer and we'll be married then. But he's running for office now and if these letters got out they'd ruin him. They'd ruin me too. I've told Dave about them; he understands. But father—well, he was a farmer and made his money in oil and he still thinks he's on a farm somewhere. A girl who'll smoke is a harlot. You can see how he'd feel about these letters."

"I have an idea," Smith said musingly.

"They were stolen from Terry. We've paid the man twice when he promised to send them back and he never has."

"Who is he?"

"We don't know. He writes me where to leave the money. I've never seen him."

Smith let his lean white hands rest flat upon the deck top. "Why are you paying instead of Terry?"

"He helped me with the first payment of five thousand, but he's lost all his money recently. I didn't let him know that I had to pay five thousand more. That took about all the cash Dave and I can get together without letting father know."

"And then somebody called up and told you I was doing the blackmailing?"

"Yes. Dave listened on the extension in his room. He swore he was coming down and kill you, but I got the only one of our cars that was in the garage and got here first."

"Which is lucky all around," Smith said. The phone jangled and he picked it up, said, "John Smith speaking."

The voice on the wire said, "Good. I called earlier but you weren't in. I've got a job for you."

It seemed to Smith that for hours that voice roared in his ears. His hands gripped telephone and receiver until his nails flattened with the pressure. The blood had jolted in his veins, and stopped.

The voice on the wire was the voice of the man who had blinded him!

FINALLY SMITH said, "Yes? What's the job?" He was afraid the other man would notice the quiver of his words, would *feel* the violence with which he held the telephone.

"There's a certain party who wants to pay me ten thousand dollars in exchange for some letters. I want you to collect the money, bring it to me, and then take the letters back to the lady. Your fee will be ten percent. Is it a go?"

"Suppose the lady isn't willing for me to be intermediary?"

"If I say so she'll be willing."

"And why are you picking on me?"

"I liked your ad in the paper. But if you're not willing to take the job, say so."

"I'll take it. Who's the lady?"

"A Miss Carol Duval. I've already called her and said that you'd act as the middleman in this transaction. She'll probably be down to see you soon."

"She's already here. There seems to have been a slight misunderstanding about what you told her."

There was short laughter. "She was probably too excited to understand. You collect the money and I'll let you know how and when to deliver it."

"Wait a minute," Smith said. "I want to talk to the lady." He put his hand over the mouthpiece, snapped at Duval, "Get out in the front office, use the other phone and have this call traced!" Then to the girl, "You heard what I said to him. He wants ten thousand more. If I deliver it. I'll bring back the letters."

"All right," she whispered. "But get them, please get them."

Smith said into the phone, "It's okay. But Miss Duval says it will take her at least four days, probably a week to collect that much cash."

The girl said, "I'll get it tomorrow! If you'll just get the letters."

"Not under four days," Smith said into the phone. "She claims she can't make it any sooner. Okay? Then you let me know."

"All right," the voice said. "And if you are trying to trace this call you're wasting your time. It's from a downtown pay station on a dial phone." The line clicked off.

John Smith hooked the receiver, his white hand moving in a slow arc through the air. He stood up. In his ears, over and over was the voice he'd heard there for ten years. But he knew that it was no accident this man had called him, no accident that the girl had misunderstood that he was to act only as an intermediary, in the blackmail. She and her brother had been sent there in the hope that they would murder him! Perhaps the robber had not forgotten the man he'd blinded, because somehow he knew how close Smith was upon his trail.

And when Smith carried the money to this man he would be walking into a planned and inescapable murder trap!

THE MOTED column of sunlight came through the dirty window. The chair with its wobbly front leg stood to the left of the sunlight. From behind the shadowed desk Lieut. Paul Rutgers' wrinkled face and black eyes looked at Smith.

"It's the only way," Smith said. "We can't convict him on the blackmail charge because the girl won't prosecute. If she's willing to pay twenty thousand dollars for those letters she's not going to voluntarily turn them over to the court. That's what makes blackmail the safest of all rackets."

"But your way's too dangerous," Rutgers said. "Somehow he's learned what you've got on him. He's looking for a chance to kill you."

"It's the only way," Smith said again. "You made me swear to keep within the law, to use proof instead of bullets. What could we do with a ten year old murder charge? Get enough evidence to ruin him socially, but not enough to convince a jury 'beyond a reasonable doubt.' There'll always be doubt about a case ten years old. We're almost sure now who the man is. He pulled me into this thing because when I began checking on Brandon and Dr. Carter, he knew I was close to him. And only one of the men close to those two has the slightest connection with Miss Duval. He's our man. But we can't prove it in court your way. This way we'll be able to convict him."

"Sure," Rutgers said. "Of your murder."

THE VOICE over the phone said. "You've got the money in your office. I'm ready for it."

Smith said, "I've been waiting, Where do you want it?"

"There's a drugstore on the corner of St. Charles and Broadway. Go there and wait. I'll telephone,"

"Okay," Smith said. "I'll be there in twenty minutes."

Royal Street, where Smith had his office, is narrow, cluttered with traffic and antique shops. The shops were closed now and despite the traffic the close-packed walls of the buildings kept the street dark. As Smith drove down it and circled on Toulouse he could feel his heart beat at his ribs, then stop for what seemed hours before it beat again. The Vieus Carré is an excellent place for murder. If the man who planned to kill John Smith tonight preferred his death to the money, then the shot might come at any time.

"I reckon he plans to get me *and* the money," Smith said as he turned Lee Circle and headed up St. Charles. But the palms of his hands were damp on the steering wheel. The night wind felt cold against his face.

It was eight thirty-five when he stopped in front of the Katz and Bestoff drugstore. For two minutes he waited, his round marblelike eyes watching as only a man who has been blind and can see again can watch. There were boys from Tulane on the sidewalk and inside the store, girls from Sophie Newcomb. Now and then cars would drive up and park, sometime in the light, sometime in the shadow. Sometimes they wanted soft drinks, sometimes a ginger ale and empty glasses.

Smith pushed open the door of his car and went inside the store. He was drinking his second coca-cola when the pay station phone rang. It was The Voice saying, "All right, there's another drugstore on Clair borne just off South Carrollton, It won't be so crowded."

When a phone call sent him from there to a third place Smith knew what was happening. The blackmailer was making sure that the detective was not being followed. He could watch Smith arrive in each place, watch everything that he did, watch him leave.

"But I wasn't being followed in the first place," Smith thought. "We might as well get on to the end."

The directions were for a deserted bathhouse on the Mississippi, the end of a road not used a dozen times a year. So the idea was to weight his body and dump it in the river. Smith thought. Well, maybe….

"From the time you leave the highway, drive without lights," the voice said. "Stop close to the boathouse, get out and walk inside. I'll meet you there."

"Okay," Smith said. "I'll be there." When he tried to wipe the perspiration from his forehead his damp hands only smeared it. "Ten years I've been waiting for this chance," he thought, "and now I'm afraid. But who the hell wouldn't be?"

THERE WAS a full half mile of road little better than a trail between the highway and the boathouse, but a full moon had come up silvering the road. Swampland shut him in on both sides. Tall gaunt and leafless trees shrouded with Spanish moss. Black water touched with ghastly patches of moonlight. Frogs and crickets that bellowed, then were still as the automobile churned past them.

The levee showed ahead, tilting up black against the sky. And hunched on the levee was the boathouse.

Smith ran his car up the levee to the very door of the house, stopped, and in the same instant had moved from under the wheel to the right side of the seat, crouching low. A full minute he sat there.

Darkness closed the door of the boathouse like a solid wall. And inside the darkness Smith could sense, could almost smell the man who waited for him. There was no movement, no sound except the farheard baying of frogs.

"Here goes," Smith thought. He pushed open the door of the car and slipped out. The moon was still low in the east so that the shadow of the automobile covered Smith until he was in the shadow of the boathouse itself. He kept close to the wall until he reached the door. The .38 revolver was in his left hand. He took a long breath and stepped through the doorway.

An overhead light crashed on with shattering and furious brilliance. The beam caught Smith like a physical blow. The rest of the place was in total darkness.

Smith was moving in the instant that the light came on, warned by a movement more sensed than heard: the lifting of an arm, the finger on a light switch. A shot crashed out while Smith was still in the air, held suspended in that beam of light like some creature under a microscope. Smith heard the hiss of the bullet past his ear even as he pulled his trigger. He had not aimed, not looked upward, but shooting as he had taught himself to shoot for ten dark years.

There was the crash of glass as the bullet struck. Darkness hurtled into the room. Smith hit the ground, rolled, and lay still. The echo of the shot dimmed against the walls and faded into silence.

For ten seconds Smith held his breath, listening. Then his left hand, holding the gun, moved until it was stretched full length from him. "You're lying down and this one will be just over your head," he said, and fired.

Flame stabbed back at him. The boom of the gun and the spank of the bullet into the wall beside Smith merged together.

Smith said, "You're holding the gun too far to your right to shoot accurately." There were two dead seconds of waiting. He said, "Quit moving your hand! I shot over you the first time. I won't again."

ACROSS THE room a man gave a choked, sobbing cry. "Who the devil are you? How can you see in the dark?"

"I was blind for ten years," Smith said. "The blind have a different kind of eyesight. If you want me to prove it I'll kill you now, but there are some things I'd rather ask you first."

"All right," the man said. "For God's sake, what do you want?"

"Are you the man who blinded me ten years ago?"

"It wasn't me!" the man said. "I swear it wasn't. It was James Brandon."

"And a month later you killed Brandon just as you had killed Jackie Crosetti. Nobody knew that you and Crosetti were acquainted and there was no danger his murder would be traced to you,"

"No," the man said. "Brandon shot him."

"And you poisoned Brandon. You had been in business together, had gone broke together. If it were known that Brandon was murdered and the police investigated, there'd been plenty of suspicion directed against you. So you hired a crooked doctor, Dr. Tom Carter, that nobody could connect you with and bribed him to say that Brandon had died of heart disease. Then after Carter left the city you followed and killed him."

"He tried to blackmail me," the man said. "He wanted more money."

There was no answer. Dead and black silence filled the room.

Four lanes of light lashed across the boathouse, centered on a short, heavy-shouldered man with the face of a mad dog. Behind one of the lights the voice of Lieutenant Paul Rutgers said, "That should be enough. Smith. I'll get a conviction all right."

The man across the room screamed, leaping to his feet, his gun swinging up. "I'll get…" the crash of three shots rumbled together in the room.

In the bright focus of light the blackmailer shuddered, went backward. The gun slipped from his fingers.

Smith said, "It's a good thing you shot, Lieutenant. With all those lights I could see him too well and so I missed."

IT WAS during the ride back to the city that Terry Carven, murderer and blackmailer and robber, turned to Smith. "How did the police get there?" he asked. "I was sure you weren't being followed.

"I wasn't," Smith said. "But nearly three weeks ago I knew I was going to find you sometime soon. You see, I knew there had been three men in that robbery where I was blinded. Lieutenant Rutgers told me that Crosetti was the only underworld character connected with the robbery, and Crosetti was murdered soon afterwards and his share of the loot disappeared. It looked as though he had been murdered by his partners to hush him up and to get his part of the money. So I figured that if the leader would kill one of his confederates for those reasons, he might kill both, be doubly safe and have more money. I knew that the man I was looking for was smart: he might have killed so cleverly that it wasn't even known to be murder. That's why I went through the newspapers getting the name of every person who had been murdered or had died in the city within two months after the time I was shot. I tried to investigate every death. I failed thirty-three times; but when I started on Brandon and learned that the doctor who testified he had died of heart disease had left the city and then been murdered, h looked as though I had something."

Carven said, "I'd been watching you, I saw you were investigating Dr. Carter and that's why I planned to get you."

"And that's where you slipped," Smith said. "It would have taken months to check on everybody who might have poisoned Brandon. At my suggestion the police dug up the body and found he had been poisoned. I suspected you because from the newspapers I learned you and he had been business partners and had lost your money at the same time. But we would never have been able to prove it. Then you called me, trying to get me out of the way, and really finished yourself. That told me, because I recognized your voice, that the man who blinded me and who murdered Brandon and Carter was the same man who was trying to blackmail Miss Duval. Only a limited number of persons knew you had those letters from her; so the blackmailer had to be one of that list. And he also had to be one of the persons who could have killed Brandon. Miss Duval could have got your money more quickly, but I needed the four days to check and learn the name of every person who knew about the letters, then compare those names with the persons who had known and associated with Brandon. You were the only one who could fit into both lists."

"Okay," Terry Carven said bitterly. "I understand how you learned who I was, but I still don't understand how the police got here. I was sure you weren't being followed."

"I wasn't," Smith said. "After we had a good idea who you were, the rest was easy. The police followed you."

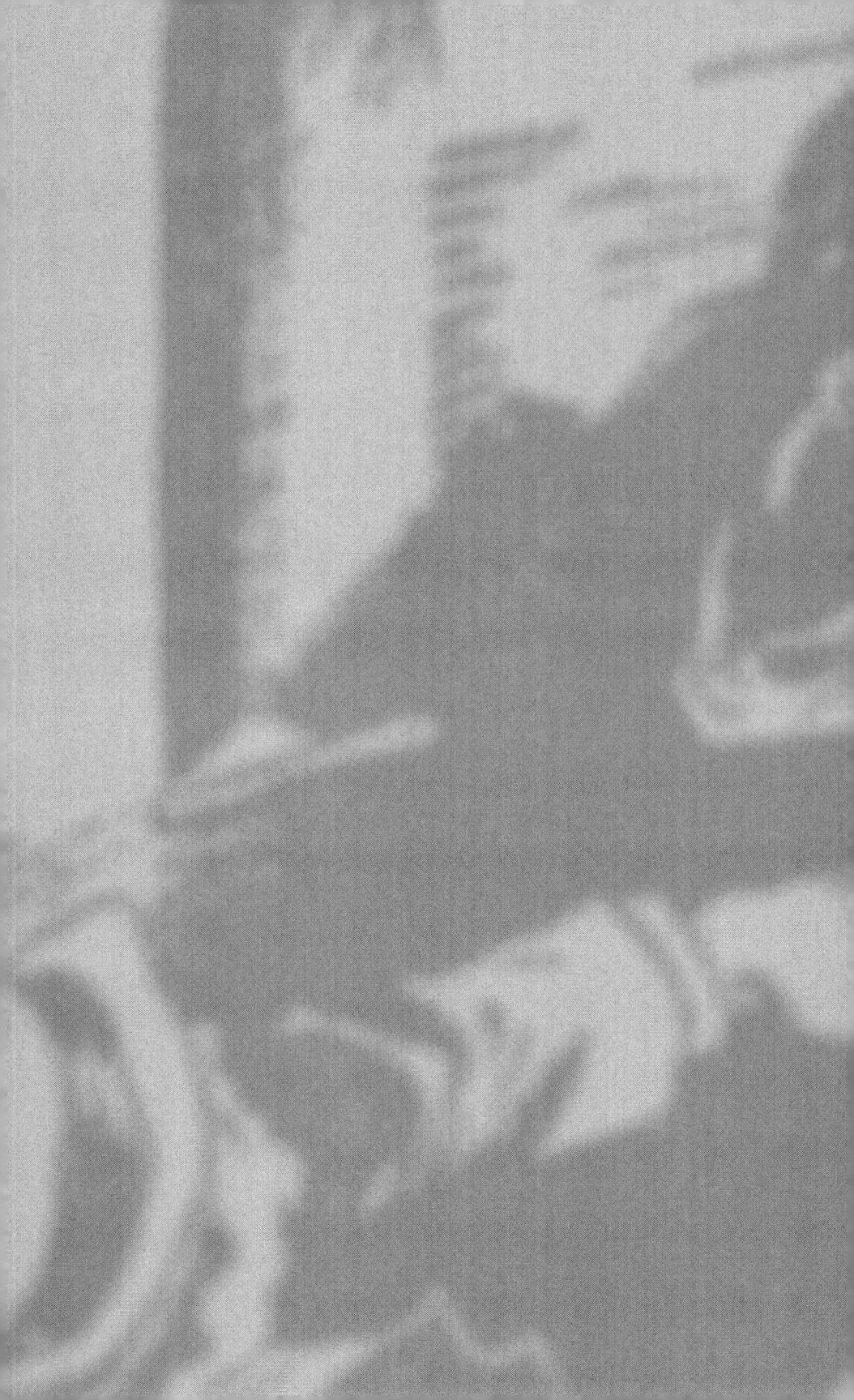

NO PAROLE FOR THE DEAD

John Smith knew of one way to beat the parole racket through which a gang-terrified parole board was saving its own hide at growing peril to the lives of honest citizens. But John Smith's method meant that he, himself, would have to verge dangerously close to the law's boundaries—that, indeed, he would have to risk his life a hundred times while his enemies risked theirs once....

CHAPTER ONE
MAN NAMED SMITH

THE SIGN above one of the innumerable antique shops on Royal Street said:

> John Smith
> Private Investigator

Most persons passed without seeing it. The sign was small and neat.

The man who glanced up at the sign was slender, but well made. He walked easily, without waste motion; moving with the restrained energy of a greyhound.

His face was in strange contrast to the virility of his body. The skin was dead white, whiter than the man's hair. It was as if he had lived for years in total darkness—which had drained the color from his face. His eyes were round and blue with a marble-like appearance such as the eyes of the blind sometimes have.

The man turned into the doorway underneath the signs. Jules Le Blanc who ran the antique shop on the first floor was standing there and said, "Howdedo, Mr. Smith. A fine afternoon isn't it?"

"Fine," Smith said. He cocked his head slightly to one side as though listening. "Bushelmouth is asleep upstairs as usual. The one thing he can do better than sleep is snore."

"How can we tell?" Le Blanc asked, then smiled and shook his head. "You sure have a remarkable pair of ears, Mr. Smith."

"Everybody could hear better if they absolutely had to," Smith said. He climbed the steps to the second floor.

The door was marked *John Smith* and the room beyond was comfortably but sparsely furnished. There were several chairs and a desk which looked small compared to the huge Negro seated behind it. Bushelmouth Johnson overflowed from his chair. His arms and legs flopped limply. His head tilted back, the mouth wide open. "He could swallow a basketball for an aspirin tablet," Smith said, and went through a second door into a small rear office.

The tommy-gun spurted flame. John Smith lay flat on the floor.

Here was another desk with one chair behind it and two in front. Smith sat behind the desk, yelled for Bushelmouth, kept yelling until the snoring stopped.

THE HUGE Negro shuffled through the door yawning. "How do, Mistur Smiff?"

"Okay, but I just had to shoot four men because you wouldn't wake up and help me fight them."

"Sho nuff?" Bushelmouth said amazed. "Whar dey co'pses?"

"I dropped them out the window," Smith said. "Been any calls for me?"

"Yossur. One gen'lemun call and he say is you heah and I say you ain't heah but you sho be heah and he say when's dat and I say mos' any time and he say well he call ag'in. But he don't soun' like he was gettin' no fun out'en it. I spec' he was scared."

"Scared?"

"He sound dat way, or else'n he got false teef."

"All right," Smith said. "Go back to sleep."

Bushelmouth went out, but a moment later his head peered around the door. "You want me to car'y off dem co'pses f'um under de window?"

"What?" Smith looked startled, then laughed. "Wait until dark. They'll keep."

It was twenty minutes later when the phone rang. A man said, "Mr. Smith? Mr. Smith is it safe to talk with you over the phone?"

Smith's blue eyes narrowed. He said, "I don't know. Where are you calling from?"

"A pay station down town."

"Anyone in the next booth?"

"No. I made certain of that."

"Then it should be safe. What do you want to talk about?"

"I can't explain now. Can you come to my home? Can you come and be absolutely certain that nobody sees you?" The man's voice was strained with fear, yet the tone retained a kind of pomposity that reminded Smith of an old fashioned Shakespearean actor or politician.

"Where is your home?"

"Twenty-five seventy-two St. Charles. Be there at ten tonight. You can name your own figure for the work. But for God's sake be certain no one sees you. Will you come?"

Five seconds dragged past before Smith answered. His eyes were very narrow, his white face pulled into a frown. He said slowly, "I'll be there."

"Good. I'll expect you." The connection snapped off.

THE ADDRESS on St. Charles was in the swank section of the city. Smith knew the city directory gave it as the home of Claude Vignaux. The frown deepened on Smith's face. He knew of Vignaux although they'd never met. One of the state's most prominent politicians. Wealthy. A member of the parole board. His son had been killed a month or so before in a night club holdup.

Perhaps that was what he wanted—and perhaps it wasn't even Vignaux who had called. And if it wasn't? The caller had asked for Smith to slip into the house unseen. "It could make a pretty picture for a frame," Smith said. "I'm a damn fool to go. But I think I will."

He spent several hours that afternoon in a newspaper morgue looking at pictures. When he left he was certain he'd recognize Claude Vignaux and most of his associates.

At eight o'clock Smith was across the street from the Vignaux home. It was a large, white-pillared place set well back from the street. Magnolias dotted the lawn, their white flowers seeming to float upon the darkness. Several lights showed dimly through curtained windows. At nine a Negro man and woman, apparently servants, went out the back. There was no other sign of life, although the lights continued to burn.

An alley ran close to the back of the Vignaux house, but Smith didn't use it. At nine fifty-five he went up the front walk of the house next door, climbed the steps and went around the porch to the side.

Once hidden by the dark he turned and stared back at the street. A trolley rumbled down the little park that marked the middle of the Avenue. Automobiles whipped past, the sound of their tires a keen whine against Smith's ears. But there was no indication of anyone watching him.

He crossed the porch and vaulted the banister. One minute later he was standing at the side of Claude Vignaux's home.

He got a window open without trouble. He didn't pause. His ears had told him nothing was breathing in this room. He went over the sill, landing inside on the balls of his feet.

It was pitch dark here. He shrugged his right shoulder slightly, feeling the weight of the gun against his ribs. His left hand was close to it as he went across the room, his right hand stretched in front of him. Twice his fingers touched chairs, but he slid around them silently, moving with an instinct like that of a blind man. Without light he found the door on the far side of the room and slid it open.

He was in a dimly illuminated hallway. There was no sound that ordinary ears could have heard, but after a moment Smith turned toward the front of the house. Outside a closed door he paused, crouching, one ear close to the panel. Only one person inside, he decided, straightened, opened the door, and stepped through. With the same motion he went sideways, so that his back was to the wall.

It was a man's study, somewhat ornately furnished. The man who stood in front of the fireplace had not heard Smith enter. He reached up, picked a highball glass off the mantel, took a swig, and turned with the glass still in his hand.

He saw Smith and made a sound as though he'd been kicked in the stomach. He stumbled back against the wall.

The glass fell from his hand, thudded on the heavy rug with a tinkling of ice and water.

Smith closed the door by which he had entered. He said, "How do you do, Mr. Vignaux?"

Claude Vignaux was a big, pompous-looking man in his early sixties with the top of his head so bald it looked as if it had been shaved. Fear shook his heavy lips when he said, "Who are you?"

"I'm John Smith. You asked me to get in without being seen."

The answer did Vignaux good. His back stiffened and he tried to smile. "You were certainly quiet about it. You startled me." Then the fear showed in his eyes again. "You're positive you weren't seen?"

"Not positive. I don't think I was."

"Let us hope not." From his breast pocket Vignaux took a handkerchief to mop at his forehead.

He left the glass on the floor, mixed two drinks from a buffet table at the side of the room, gave one to Smith. He waved the younger man toward a heavy leather-cushioned chair and took a seat opposite him. He drank deeply, said as though about to plunge into cold water, "I might as well get to it."

Smith said, "Okay." He held the glass in his right hand, sipping it, keeping the elbow well away from his body so that the gun under his coat wasn't crowded.

"I've made inquiries about you, Mr. Smith. What I have to say is, well…. If it were overheard I wouldn't live long and probably you wouldn't either. Do you want me to go ahead?"

Smith took a mouthful of scotch and soda, held it a moment to savor the flavor. It was excellent. He said, "Go ahead."

"I can phrase it very simply," Vignaux said. "I want you to smash the parole racket."

CHAPTER TWO
RACKET BUSTER

VIGNAUX'S FACE grew hard, determination stamping out the fear which had shown there. "I have served on the parole board of this state for more than a year," he said slowly. "Just how many criminals I have voted to parole, to turn back into society, I don't know. Three months ago I voted to parole Sam Musik. A month ago Musik and Little Johnnie Johnson and Rodello held up the Crescent Club. You read about it?"

"Yes, I read something about it."

"They got away with several thousand dollars in cash and God knows how much in jewels. They killed two men and a woman getting away."

Vignaux paused. His big hands knotted. He said, "One of those men was my son." Smith sat so still that even the ice did not tinkle in his glass. The Crescent holdup was only one in a mad series of crimes by Sam Musik and his killers, a series which had begun soon after Musik's last parole. The police had tried frantically to run them down, and had failed. The killers appeared, murdered, robbed, and vanished.

"The first thing I want you to do," Vignaux said, "is get Sam Musik, Johnson, and Rodello. But I don't want you to stop there. I want you to keep on."

"How?"

Vignaux came to his feet. His face was grim. "You know the results of the parole system in this country, Mr. Smith.

The system was intended to help men who were really worthy. Sometimes it does. But more often it works the other way. Musik, Johnson, Rodello are all out of prison on parole. It's the second time for Musik and Johnson. But that's nothing unusual. John Dillinger was a paroled convict. Pretty Boy Floyd was on parole and so was Adam Richetti when they shot down four officers trying to rescue Frank Nash. Nash also had been paroled. Baby Face Nelson killed three G-men—after his *third* parole. The records are full of things like that."

Smith said, "Why?"

"Politics," Vignaux said. He swallowed heavily. "I knew Sam Musik was a killer when I voted for his parole. So did the other members on the board."

"Then why turn him free?"

"Because," Vignaux said, "we were told to. I don't know who heads the parole racket in this state. Whoever it is, the Governor, the senators, the congressmen do what they're told. Probably they don't know any more than I do who's back of it. But when the word comes down that So-and-So should be paroled—he gets parole."

"And if he doesn't?"

"Something happens to the man who opposed it. Maybe he only loses his job. Maybe he disappears. Maybe he dies accidentally. You remember Tom Conners who was drowned when his sail boat overturned? Beauchamp who was killed in a highway accident? Farman who was murdered without apparent reason?"

Very softly Smith said, "I remember."

HIS BLUE eyes were wide now and behind them his brain rushed swiftly. For the first time he was realizing what a gigantic thing the parole racket could be. If one man could control the granting of paroles he could practically force the underworld to cut him in on all its profits, and do all his dirty work. He could force his way into the semi-legal political graft. His power and money would be limitless.

"And you?" Smith said.

Vignaux said, "I did like the others: I did as I was told. And last month my son was killed, murdered, by a man I voted to free. *I killed my son by that vote!*"

Smith did not speak. He sat motionless, holding the highball glass, waiting.

"I'm responsible for other murders," Vignaux went on. "For every one that Musik and Johnson and Rodello commit. Now I'm going to do what I can to make up for it. The police are helpless. An outsider can do more. I'll pay."

"It's a big job," Smith said.

"I've money. Lots of it."

Smith said, "I wasn't thinking of money." He stood up, crossed the room, soundless on the heavy rug, and turned. He said, "Ten and a half years ago I blundered into a bank holdup and one of the robbers bounced a bullet off my skull. For ten years I was blind, until an operation gave me back my sight. I learned things in those years: how to move in the dark, how to use my ears as normal persons never have to learn, how to shoot at sound rather than sight. Even now I'm a better shot when I don't see the thing. But mainly, sitting there in the dark, not knowing whether or not I'd ever see again, I learned to hate crime."

"I was told that," Vignaux said, "That's why I came to you."

"There's another side to it. I don't have experience. I got the man who blinded me. I've had one or two small cases. That's all. This is big. I may fail."

Vignaux said, "Failure can mean but one thing: Death. The entire underworld will be against you. If anyone learns what you're after, you won't last an hour. And it's not the underworld alone you'll be dealing with."

Smith said, "I'll try."

His eyes narrowed slightly, head cocked to one side. He said sharply, "where's your wife?"

"Why—er—she's out tonight. Should be back about now."

"She's unlocking the front door," Smith said. "At least, someone is."

"But how… how…?" Vignaux stared at him amazed.

"A man who's blind learns to use his ears," Smith said.

He pocketed the ten one-hundred dollar bills Vignaux had placed on the desk. A moment later Mrs. Vignaux began to call, "Claude, where are you?"

DETECTIVE LIEUTENANT Paul Rutgers was small and wizened and dark. He wasn't a brilliant cop but he was thorough. And he was honest. Over his desk top he regarded Smith with eyes that were coal black and without luster. He said, "I'm a cop. I can't sanction anybody getting outside the law."

Smith's white hands rested on the desktop. His white face was pushed forward above them. "When you gave me my license," he said, "I promised to stay inside the law. I'll do it. But if I come too much into the open, I won't last. And if I get the police as well as the crooks after me, I won't last."

"What are you planning?"

"To do it the only way it can be done. Newspapers have been whooping about the parole system for years—on their editorial pages. But nobody reads the editorial pages. I'm going to make the parole system a front page story. Once the people get really aroused crooked politicians can't stop them."

"If they ever get aroused," Rutgers said bitterly.

"They will be. But I'll need help. The first thing I want is some information about Eddie Brietz. I've been told that he and Sam Musik used to be pals."

"Used to be," Rutgers said. "Bosom pals before Musik got tough. He wouldn't speak to a rat like Brietz now. Eddie is out on parole himself. Housebreaking is his limit. He's got the guts of a pigeon. But we pulled him in and worked him over trying to get some dope on Musik. He doesn't have any. And nobody else seems to."

"I'll try him," Smith said.

Eddie Brietz was little. He had the pinched face of a rat and eyes that trembled like palsied hands. He looked ready to jump and run. He had black hair that he wore slicked tight and clothes padded in the shoulders until he was shaped like an inverted triangle. When there was a good-looking woman in sight he strutted.

Smith found him in a bar on Decatur Street and for two days clung tight to his trail. The break came on the second night. Brietz met a large flat-nosed man in a dump out on St. Ann Street and retired to one of the private dining rooms at the rear. Smith, standing at the far end of the bar, watched them go.

It wasn't the sort of place you take the children for ice cream. One bartender was Greek, one Cajan. Together they weighed over four hundred pounds. There were four men and two women at the bar. Smith's eyes, that blindness had taught to see, found gun-bulges on two of the men. "The others probably have knives," he thought.

Smith finished his beer and pushed the glass back across the bar to the Cajan. "Any shrimp?" he asked.

"Plenty. They come thes' morning, yes."

"Creole style," Smith said.

The Cajan disappeared toward the kitchen. The Greek was busy drawing a beer. Smith strolled toward a door in the rear marked, "Men." It was just beyond this that a swinging door led into the private dining rooms where Brietz and his flat-nosed companions had gone.

SMITH LET the washroom door close behind him. One swift glance told him the place was empty. He looked for a door into the dining room but there wasn't any.

He cracked the door open and looked out. The customers were sideways to him. The Greek was bent over a beer spigot. Smith ducked out and through the swinging door to the left.

He was in a narrow hall with private stalls to right and left. Voices muttered beyond the third door on the right and Smith opened the second one softly, pampered it close behind him. On the balls of his feet he crossed to the wall and knelt with one ear against it.

The men were talking in whispers, but the walls were thin. The words came clear to Smith's ears.

"It sounds too damn good, Eddie. Like a frame. You cross me, and I'll tear you apart."

"Listen, Nick." Brietz' voice was a whine. "You know I wouldn't rat on you."

"Not and live," Nick said.

"It's just like I told you. Old man Jerpsun's gone to Baton Rouge and the old woman with him. There's not a servant in the house. If you've taken care of the watchman…."

"He's off on a brawl," Nick said, "And won't know what a hangover he's goin' to have till tomorrow—*if* he wakes up then."

"But there's the guy who's been tailing me for two days," Brietz said. "I swear I don't know what he wants. He ain't a cop and he don't know much. He's stuck to me like a poodle. He's out in the bar now."

"You're sure you don't know who he is?" There was the scrape of shoes and a thump as though Nick had reached across the table, grabbed Brietz and jerked him forward.

"I swear! I like you, Nick. I wouldn't cross you."

"All right," Nick said. "We can fix this guy. There's an alley half way down the block. Let him follow you past that. Then we'll get on out to Jerpsun's. And if you cross me…."

Smith was listening so intently that at first he paid no attention to the sound behind him. And then he heard it again, the soft whisper of a man tiptoeing along the hall. The step came again, just outside his door. The knob began to turn.

The Greek's head and shoulders came through. His right hand was raised shoulder high. In it was a blackjack.

CHAPTER THREE
BEER ON ST. ANN'S

JOHN SMITH had moved like a dancer, coming erect, spinning high on his toes. His right shoulder was against the wall and a foot from the door when it opened. His left hand had dipped under his coat and came out holding a .38 police special. Standing on his toes put him almost level with the Greek's head. He swung his gun.

There was a dull crack as it landed and a low *whoosh* of air from the Greek's open mouth. His knees buckled. His hand wobbled slowly downward, still holding the blackjack.

With his right hand Smith caught the blackjack, then grabbed the Greek with both arms. It felt as though he were trying to prop up the Washington monument, but he managed to get the body quietly on the floor. In the next room the voices of Brietz and Nick flowed on without interruption.

Smith put his gun in its holster, the blackjack in his pocket. The Greek's feet stuck out the door into the hallway. When Smith pulled them inside they slid out again. He pulled them back and braced them against the wall. Then he stepped out into the hall and closed the door behind him.

He went into the barroom again, his face blank but every muscle in his body pulled rigid. No one noticed when he entered. The Cajan was ready with the creoled shrimp. He paid no attention when Smith wandered to a phone at the end of the bar.

When Bushelmouth answered Smith's ring the Cajan was standing close by. Smith didn't know whether or not he was listening. He said, "Hello, baby. You going to be busy about an hour from now?"

Bushelmouth Johnson said, "Which who? Dis de Jawn Smiff Aguncy."

"Good," Smith said. "Get your best robes on, darling. I'm going to be off work in an hour or so. I'll pick you up."

"Hit's you, Mistur Smiff! Whar you drinkin'? Maybe Ah better come drive yo' car."

Smith said, "Listen, sweetheart. How about...." The Cajan drifted toward the other end of the bar. The insipid smile on Smith's face didn't change, but the tone of his voice did. He snapped, "A bar at St. Ann's and Dupre. Rush. Come in, tell me I've got to go to Algiers in a hurry. Rush it or I'll break your Goddamned neck." And while Bushelmouth was sputtering he said, more loudly, "See you then, babe," and hung up.

Back at his place at the bar he began to eat shrimp. He heard the Cajan ask where the Greek bartender had gone. A man shrugged toward the toilet.

Smith ate with his right hand, a little awkwardly. He kept his left hand free and near the lapel of his coat. And without appearing to, he watched the door toward the private dining rooms.

That Greek wouldn't stay out long. His skull was too solid. If he regained consciousness now hell would break loose. But if Smith left Brietz and Nick might suspect that he was still tailing them and call off the burglary. Smith needed that burglary in his plans.

He was half through his shrimp when Eddie Brietz and Nick came past the swinging door into the barroom. In the mirror back of the bar Smith saw the little man nod toward him, heard Nick whisper, "Okay."

And then Bushelmouth Johnson crashed the front door. He went at Smith with a rush, yelling, "You got to go to Algiers! Dhat's what you said. And I'm tellin'...."

SMITH SPUN on the seat and dived. He hit Bushelmouth in the chest with both hands, jarring the last words out of him. "Algiers!" he shouted. "Come on!"

"Yessur. Dat's what you...."

But Smith had left a bill on the bar and pushed Bushelmouth out the door. From the sidewalk he looked back and caught a glimpse of Nick grinning after him. Then he was across the street and in his automobile.

"You better let me drive, Mistur Smiff," Bushelmouth said. "Course you ain't drunk. But maybe you's a little daisy an'...."

"I've had two beers," Smith said. "I just wanted those gentlemen to think I'm going where I'm not. You almost muffed it, but at that you did better than I expected." He dug a dollar out of his pocket and handed it over. "Invest in some Bay Saint Louis Corn," he said.

Bushelmouth said, "Hotdamn! Dis legal liquor ain't got no mule in it. Taste to me like dishwater and rubbin' alcohol." He was quiet for a moment, then turned on the seat to face Smith. His face was puckered with worry. "Ah couldn't find 'em," he said.

Smith said, "Find who?"

"Them co'pses."

"What the hell are you talking about?"

"Them you throw'd out'm de window two days ago. I jest thought 'bout 'em while ago and figerred dey was fixin' to smell so's I went out to car'y'm off. And I couldn't find 'em."

Smith said, "Oh God." He shook his head, said, "Don't worry about them. I carried them away myself."

"But ain't...."

"Just forget it," Smith said. He pulled to the curb and stopped. "Go on and get your liquor. I've work to do."

Arthur Jerpsun's home was ten miles beyond the city limits on the Baton Rouge highway. It was a vast, ornate place, set a half mile back from the road. Smith drove to within a quarter of a mile, hid his car back of a clump of blackjack and sassafras bushes, and went the rest of the way on foot.

There was a chance that Brietz would not turn up. He might have seen through Smith's ruse, or the Greek bartender might have regained consciousness before Brietz and Nick left. All Smith could do was wait. He jimmied a window open, crawled through, and closed the window behind him.

He did not use a light, yet he moved fairly swiftly. He found a bottle of scotch in the kitchen, then ice, made a large drink, and headed back for the living room. He groped about for the most comfortable chair, put an ash tray beside it, lighted a cigaret, and waited.

In the utter stillness Smith heard the men before they reached the house. He didn't move except to crush out his cigaret, to sip at his drink.

Brietz and Nick went to work on the window in the next room. Smith heard wood grind under metal, the window latch snap. He kept drinking, tilting the glass slowly so that the ice didn't tinkle. There was the scuffle of shoes on wood as a man climbed through the open window. Smith finished his drink, put the glass down and stood up.

In the next room Nick said, "Keep your damned eyes open."

From outside Brietz said, "It's like having the old guy mail it to us. The safe's in the next room."

"And if this combination don't work," Nick said, "You and that maid girl-friend of yours are both going to get your faces bashed."

Brietz's voice was a kind of whine. He said. "It'll work. Hell, they don't lie to me."

"You better hope not," Nick said.

IN HIS first tour of the room Smith had placed every object. He crossed now, circling a chair and table as if he could see them. He was close to the connecting door when a flashlight went on in the next room. The light tunneled through the door within inches of Smith's shoulder. There was the pad of steps and the cone of light grew smaller as the flash neared the door.

Smith pulled his gun from its holster with his left hand, balanced it. He saw the tip of Nick's right shoe cross the door-sill, the point of the flashlight. He was holding the light with his right hand, a slip of paper with his left. Both were gloved.

He took one step past the door, then Smith leaned out and let him have it. The blow seemed to explode him forward and he went over on his face with a crash.

Even while he fell Smith was moving. One jump put him in the next room and another carried him to the window. Brietz's rat face was peering in at darkness, too startled by the sudden noise to move. Smith jabbed the gun muzzle between his eyes. "Okay, Eddie," he said. "Come on in."

His original plan had been to catch Brietz in the act of robbery, use that as a weapon to force him to talk. But he had a better idea now. He dragged Brietz into the room. "So you double-crossed a pal," he snapped. "Nick'll tear you apart for this."

Brietz went down on his knees. "God! You can't do that. He'll kill me. And I ain't...."

"Maybe you ain't," Smith said. "But so help me God if you don't talk I'll make him believe you put the finger on him. And I'll lock you in the room with him."

"He'll kill me!" Brietz sobbed.

Smith said, "All right. Then talk fast. Where's Sam Musik?"

Brietz pawed at him and Smith slashed him with the gun knocking him away. "I don't know," Brietz cried. "I swear I don't know."

Smith hit him again, gently but so the sight of his gun cut flesh. Brietz began to sob. "The police beat you worse than that," Smith said. "You didn't crack for them, and I'm not going to waste time on you. I'll let Nick do the work for me."

"But I don't know where Sam is. I swear! I haven't seen him for months!"

Smith grabbed him by the collar. "Come on. I'm going to handcuff you to Nick and leave you."

Brietz grabbed him around the knees. "Musik'll kill me if I talk about him! You know he will! I won't stand a chance!"

"That's why you wouldn't talk to the police," Smith said. "I'm no cop. Musik won't know what you tell me. But if you prefer that chance to being left with Nick…." He began to drag Brietz toward the door.

Brietz yowled, "Wait! All I know is Sam used to have a hangout about three blocks east of the French Market. Over 'round Mandeville or Spain Streets. It was right around there, but I don't know exactly. I swear I don't."

Smith hit him, dragging the gun sight across his face. "Come on," he said. "Where was it?"

"I don't know! I don't know!" The man was blubbering now. He was telling the truth and Smith knew it.

CHAPTER FOUR
FRONT PAGE PICTURES

S**MITH SAID,** "Okay. What does Musik eat?"

"Eat?"

"Yeah, eat," Smith said. "That's the one thing a man's got to do, no matter where he is. What does he eat and what does he drink?"

"He—he just eats like other guys."

Smith's hand tightened on Brietz's collar until his knuckles punched into flesh. "I mean what does he like better than anything. What does he eat every day, twice a day maybe?"

"Anchovies," Brietz said. "I swear he does. He eats a tube of anchovy paste every day. He's crazy. Sometimes he'll eat two if he's got a job coming up an's nervous. He lives on the stuff."

Twice Smith had heard Nick stir in the next room, move with returning consciousness. He'd paid no attention except to speed his questions, trying to jerk his information out of Brietz before the other man came to. Through the last questions there had been a period of silence during which Nick had not moved at all.

And then Nick moved fast. Smith heard the click of a gun coming out of its holster catch, the scrape of metal on leather. There was no time to jump right or left for the shelter of the door. His legs flew out from under him and he came down with a crash close to Brietz. Gunfire shook the next room. Flame stabbed the darkness. Smith felt the *whipp* of wind over his head as he fell.

Brietz screamed. He tried to jump aside but Smith's right hand was still in his collar, holding him. In the next room Nick fired again. Smith felt Brietz shudder and smash forward against him. The scream broke into a throaty gurgle. Brietz's head drooled over Smith's shoulder and after a moment blood started to drip from his mouth.

Nick fired for the third time in four seconds. Brietz was still making gurgling sounds when the bullet caught him. It jarred Smith off balance and his own shot smashed into the wall. He kept still then, crouched in darkness, holding Brietz to him with his right hand, his gun in his left.

The noise shook out of the rooms and a quiet as thick as the darkness came into it. Smith's head cocked slightly. The gun in his left hand moved as though turned by some electrical and automatic connection with his ears. He said, "Drop your gun, Nick. I'm warning you."

Nick fired. Smith, huddled back of Brietz, did not even see the flash. He fired twice at the point where he'd heard Nick breathing. There was a choked, coughing cry that mingled with the rumble of the guns, the jar of a body which had been crouched on all fours falling face down, the thud of a gun, the bird-like flutter of hands against a rug.

And then silence.

For twenty seconds Smith did not move. The shots might have attracted attention and he had to hurry, but he didn't stand up until his ears told him that Nick was not breathing.

He went through the house until he found the reception room and switched on the light. The huge chandelier made the place white and dazzling. Smith pulled a table into the center of the floor, placed a chair on each side of it. In one he put the body of Nick and in the other the body of Eddie Brietz. Both had been shot through the chest.

Their mouths were open. Blood streamed down across their chins.

In another room Smith found paper and pen. He printed in large letters:

> POLITICS PAROLED A CRIMINAL
> BUT DEATH GIVES NO PAROLE

With a carving knife he pinned the message to Brietz's chest.

On the table between the two men he piled the jewels they had come to steal, using the combination Nick had written down to open the safe. Then he stepped back and looked at them under the blazing light of the chandelier. "That should make a front page picture," he said aloud.

HE TELEPHONED police head-quarters and asked for Rutgers. When the lieutenant was on the line he said, "It's all been perfectly legal. Lieutenant. Or almost all of it."

"What are you talking about?"

"Come on out to Arthur Jerpsun's place," Smith said. "And bring the newspaper boys with you, photographers and all. You'd better tell them that you had a tip Eddie Brietz and a man named Nick—"

"A big guy with a flat nose?" Rutgers asked. "That'll be Nick Crass."

"—And Nick Crass were going to rob Jerpsun's tonight. You sent a man out to watch. He arrested Brietz but Crass opened fire, killing Brietz who was standing in front of your detective. Your man killed Crass. But the phone was out of order and he had to go down the road to call. Before he got back—some unknown character slipped in and left the bodies in a rather spectacular position. That'll be your story for the newspapers anyway. And incidentally, one of the maids furnished Brietz with a combination to the safe."

Rutgers began to sputter questions but Smith said, "And about Nick Crass. Had he ever had a parole?"

"One a year ago," Rutgers said. "But...."

Smith said, "Bring the newspaper boys with you," and hung up.

He went back to the message pinned on Brietz's chest, scratched out the word "A" and printed above it "TWO." He added an "S" to CRIMINAL.

Next he pulled the phone wire loose. That would help Rutgers story to the papers. But it wouldn't fool the underworld. They'd know the police were covering some outside character. And tomorrow the whole criminal world would begin a death search for the man who wrote the message that death gives no parole.

He left the light in the reception room blazing, going out of the window which Nick had entered. From behind a clump of shrubs two hundred yards away he watched until the police and newspapermen arrived.

He stood up, a small man with a face so white it seemed a blur against the darkness. There were tired lines at the corners of his blue eyes. Muscle bunched on his jaws. "That should be enough for tonight," he said aloud. "I'm going to get some sleep. Tomorrow I'll see about Sam Musik."

The morning papers went hysterical. They carried streamers and front page pictures. They ran whole inside pages of pictures taken from every conceivable angle. And though the police said things had happened just as Rutgers claimed and that the case was closed, the papers played up the angle of the mystery-man who had arranged the bodies and pinned his message to one of them with a silver knife.

And that same morning Sam Musik, Rodello, and Little Johnnie Johnson struck again. A bank messenger was murdered on Canal Street, his hand chopped off to get the bag which he carried chained to his wrist. The killers had roared off into the French Quarter, and vanished.

WHEN THE murder took place John Smith was posing as a salesman of anchovy paste. He started at the river two blocks east of the French Market and worked north for six blocks. He went into every store on the street, asking about how much they sold, whether or not there had been any increase recently. And quite casually he would mention that sometimes a person would become abnormally fond of it and eat more than a hundred average persons.

On the second day he found a merchant who agreed with him. "Now there's a lady like that in the neighborhood," the merchant said. "Moved in about a month ago. She's in here every other day for three or four tubes of anchovy paste. Sometimes she buys it by the box. She must live on it."

"Really!" Smith said. "As a rule that sort of thing isn't good for a person. It makes them skinny and sallow and puts pimples on their faces."

The merchant said, "Hummpp. Nothing like that to this baby. She's got curves where they ought to be and if she got any pimples they ain't where they show. She's a honey. Red-headed."

"You can't ever tell," Smith said, and wandered out. His face showed no emotion, but he could feel the increase of his heart beat, excitement tightening around his lungs like a wire. Naturally Sam Musik and his killers could not wander about buying food, but their women could. And

Musik had always showed a preference for red-headed women!

Luck was with Smith. Late that same afternoon from his stand across the street he saw a red-haired woman turn into the delicatessen. "That's her," he said tightly. The stamp of the gunmoll was on her. She was a honey all right, but hard.

Smith crossed the street, moving faster than he seemed to. For a moment he stopped in front of the store, apparently inspecting the fruits in the window. They didn't please him and he started off, but not before he'd seen the anchovy paste the merchant was handing the woman!

Thirty yards away he turned into a drugstore for a cocacola. Through the window he watched the red-haired girl go by. Her curves were all in the proper places, and the tight-fitting dress she wore called attention to them. "It's a wonder he has time for all those anchovies," Smith thought.

He finished the drink and sauntered out to the walk. The sun had dropped to where it seemed to block the end of the street, and Smith grinned crookedly at the silhouette which tempted him to follow closely on the heels of the lady he wanted. But he had made a blunder in tailing one person, and he learned by experience.

The red-head went in and out of several stores. She circled the block. Now and then she glanced back as though to make certain no one followed. As a rule Smith was on the opposite side of the street, apparently unaware of her altogether. He felt positive she hadn't spotted him.

He trailed her for thirty minutes before she stopped in front of a three-storied brick building that sat flush against the walk. It was a barnlike place with a sign "Rooms" hung in front. A heavy line had been drawn through the sign to show that the place was fully occupied.

The woman stood for a moment glancing about her, then went up the steps swiftly. The door opened before she reached it, closed behind her.

SMITH'S HEART beat a one-two and he said, "Hotdamn!" without actually moving his lips. Here was the hideout of Sam Musik and his two killers, a hideout which the police had sought frantically for weeks. And here were the men that Smith was seeking—here was a chance to really smear the papers with headlines about parole!

But there were three men in that house, swift and deadly men with guns. There was at least one woman, probably three. And you don't have to be very big to pull a trigger.

It would be suicide to go after them alone. But if he called in the police what chance would there be to make headlines about parole?

And if he didn't call in the police? His parole campaign would end completely with his death. Musik and his killers would probably escape to continue their murders and pillaging.

"It'll have to be the police," he thought. "And I'll take what chance I can on headlines afterwards."

He strolled on past the house, apparently paying it no attention. It had a deserted, empty look despite the sign which said all the rooms were occupied. There were no lights showing at all. The front door was solid and closed tight.

Just beyond the house a narrow alley emptied on the sidewalk. It was almost dark now and in the alley the shadows were purple and black. From across the street it would have been impossible to see the man who crouched there. The gloom gave no shimmer of light on the long-barreled target pistol that he held. There was a Maxim silencer fitted on the muzzle, giving the gun an awkward, blunderbus appearance.

The man crouched at the very mouth of the alley, hidden from Smith by the side of the house itself. There was no one else in the block. Smith's rubber-soled shoes made little noise. The man strained his ears for the sound of them, and waited.

CHAPTER FIVE
FIRE ESCAPE TO HELL

SMITH CAME past the front of the house. He saw the alley and thought the police would probably bottle it up when they arrived. It might be through this alley that Musik and Johnson and Rodello planned to make emergency exits. He was thinking that as he stepped past the mouth of the alley.

The man in the shadows moved with slow deliberation. He straightened from his crouching position. His elbow bent, bringing the gun up carefully. He fired.

Smith did not see the movement, but he heard the deep intake of breath with which the man had straightened. He heard the creek of shoe leather as the man shifted his weight. He leaped, spinning, his left hand slicing under his coat and out again.

The bullet caught him high in the left shoulder as he spun, whipping him around like a top. There was a glimpse of a flat, nose-smeared face that he recognized as Rodello's. He tried to shoot, but the muscles of his left hand were abnormally stiff. The gun slid out of his fingers.

Still spinning Smith dived, rolling sideways, using his hips like a blocking halfback. His body caught Rodello just over the knees. They went down with a sudden crash.

Smith hit rolling. He felt something jar lightly against his right side and remembered the blackjack he'd taken from the Greek two nights before. He got it out with his right hand.

Rodello was coming up on all fours. He tried to rock back, taking both hands off the ground, bringing up his right so that he could fire. There was no pain in Smith's left arm, no time for it although the hand seemed to move with slow numbness. He caught the large muzzle of the silencer and pushed it down. The movement pulled Rodello's head toward him.

Smith swung the blackjack. He hadn't known before how hard he could hit with his right hand. Rodello flattened, lay still.

Smith got his gun. There was pain in his shoulder now and his left hand worked better. He could feel the warm flow of blood down his arm as he reached for his gun. A flesh wound, he figured.

He stood up, looking around him. There was no one on the street and the fight had been so close to the house that the slight bulge along the front wall hid them from any of the windows. The struggle had been practically silent except for the muffled *phutt* of the silenced gun.

There was no time now to wonder how Musik and his killers had learned that Smith was after them. But they knew, and he'd have to worry about the *how* later. What mattered was Musik and Little Johnnie Johnson would wait only a few minutes for Rodello to come back. When he didn't they'd know something was wrong, and scram.

There was no chance now to go for the police. He had to tackle them alone.

THE BUILDING was old fashioned with water pipes and electric wires along the outside. A fire-escape five yards down the alley, the ladder pulled down from the bottom landing, showed how Rodello had reached the alley. The others must be on the second or third floor, Smith reasoned, or there'd been no need to use the fire-escape.

He dragged Rodello against the wall, handcuffed him to the waterpipe. That would take care of him. But how could he cover both the fire-escape and the front exit from the house?

And then he saw his chance in the electric light wires which ran along the side of the building.

He scooped up the silenced gun and moved toward the fire-escape swiftly. Anyone looking out the windows could see him now, but he had to chance that. He climbed the ladder four steps to where the light wires were level with his head. His left arm hurt like hell. He could feel his pulse pounding.

The wire was old, bare patches showing through the insulation every few inches. He hooked his arm through the fire-escape, caught one of the insulated parts, then pushed the muzzle of the silenced gun close to the bare wire. He fired.

One end of the wire fell to touch against the fire-escape, but Smith held the other end free. He kept pushing it away from the ladder until he was on the ground again, then dropped the bare end against the iron. That would complete the circuit and send one hundred and ten volts up and down the fire-escape. That wasn't a deadly charge under most circumstances but it would be a hell of a surprise to anyone who touched it.

He raised the silenced gun and fired one more shot, pausing to make sure it hit what he wanted. Then he was on the front walk running. He knew the door would be locked and tried a window. It was fastened, but the thin steel jimmy he'd used at Jerpsun's got it open and he went inside.

He could hear the dull mutter of voices from the rear and upstairs though he couldn't understand what was being said. But there was a muted note of excitement. Probably they were getting worried about Rodello. It wouldn't be long now before things broke.

There was only one stairway, beginning about halfway down the front hall. Smith sprawled flat on his belly in the living-room, his head at the corner of the door and hallway where he could watch the stair.

A door opened upstairs. A man said, "Damnit, he should have been back. Go down and see, Johnnie."

Steps moved along to the head of the stairway and started down. Smith watched feet, knees, legs come into view. Little Johnnie Johnson had been named with sarcasm. He was six feet two and pushed the scales above the two hundred mark. He had a chest that almost blocked the stairway. A .45 automatic looked small in his hand. And finally his face was visible.

Smith said, "Drop the gun. We have the place surrounded."

Johnson began to fire. The first two bullets smashed into the front door before he even saw Smith. Before he could shoot again Smith did. Johnson rocked backward, then forward, bending over at the middle. The automatic began fast, jerking thunder. Johnson kept bending until his head was below his waist and he fell. He came over and over down the stairway, still firing. When he hit the bottom it shook the house. The gun bounced out of his hand and he lay still.

There was too much rolling noise for Smith to hear the snapped orders upstairs. Then a woman screamed, an inhuman, horrible sound that ripped upward and broke. In the shocked, quivering silence that followed someone cried, "My God! She's electrocuted!" Feet stumbled across a room.

Musik's voice had a throaty shaking sound. "I'm going downstairs. That way'll burn us all—we won't have a chance."

HIS FEET showed at the top of the stair. And at the same instant a submachine gun began its blasting roar. Bullets tore at the doorjam within inches of Smith's face, ripped splinters from the floor. He fired once at charging feet and missed. A splinter slashed him on the forehead, made his finger jerk at the trigger and he knew he'd missed again.

Musik was in full view halfway down the stairs. A lean, bony, high-cheeked face with sunken eyes, and a twisted mouth. For one instant he and Smith looked at each other. It was an instant in which the submachine gun was not firing. Musik swung it slightly and squeezed the trigger. Its roar drowned out the single crack of Smith's revolver.

Musik was moving too fast to stop. He seemed to outrun his feet, his body going out in front of him. And then, without ever touching the bottom eight steps he came down on Johnson's body.

There were two women on the stair, both with guns. The red-head and a brunette. They stopped firing when Musik fell, hesitated, then flung their guns to the hall below them.

Smith stood up. "Come on, ladies," he said.

On the sudden quiet the wail of a police siren was earsplitting. Another joined it, not more than a block away. They'd be here within two minutes.

Smith yelled, "Come on down!" He grabbed the brunette by the wrist and jerked. Her high heel caught the edge of the step and she fell, landing face down on Musik and Johnson. Smith grabbed for the red-head.

She said, "You louse," and struck at him.

He didn't have time to waste. He caught her arms, pulled and helped with a light tap of his revolver on the back of her head. She piled onto the others at the foot of the stair. He grabbed a couple of silken ankles, grinning despite himself, and cuffed them together with the cuff running through the banisters. That didn't stop the noise they were making, but it would keep them face down on the dead men.

There wasn't time to search for paper. He broke the point of his fountain pen smearing the words in huge black letters on the wall above the pile of living and dead.

Crooked Politicians Freed These Murderers But
DEATH GIVES NO PAROLE

A police car had stopped out front and the brakes of another were making banshee noise. The redhead and brunette looked indecent and sounded that way. Smith said, "Goodness gracious, what language!" and went racing up the stair. The police had the front blocked.

In the room above the fire-escape a woman, nude except for a light bathrobe, lay sprawled half in the window, half out on the fire-escape. A pool of water had dripped from her body to the floor. She had jumped out of the bath at the first sound of shots, grabbed the robe, and leaped for the window. Wet, the shock had been greater than otherwise, but probably the surprise and fright had done as much to stop her heart as the electricity.

Smith swung a chair to the window sill, took aim and dropped it. A leg caught the electric wire and pulled one end free of the fire-escape. Then he was outside without ever touching the corpse and going swiftly downward.

Over the telephone Lieutenant Rutgers said, "You saw what the papers did with the story. You're getting parole on the front pages all right. And the department is getting credit for catching a lot of criminals. We didn't know when we got a call to send a radio car because a stray bullet had come through a window that we were going to run in on a pile of corpses."

"I figured I'd need help," Smith said, "and I didn't have time to call for it myself. So I threw one of those silent bullets through a window across the street, then managed to take care of everything myself."

Rutgers said, "You certainly did. And the dames talked. The black-headed one says she was tailing the red-head to make sure nobody else followed her. You were almost back to the house when she realized you were tailing the red-head, and alone. So she highballed up and told Musik. Musik didn't want to scram unless he had to, so he sent Rodello out to get you."

"That's the way it was, huh?" Smith said. "I didn't think the red-head knew I was following."

"The girl on the fire-escape was dead," Rutgers said. "And Rodello almost was. You didn't know that the water pipe you cuffed him to touched the fire-escape."

"That'll give him a taste of how the chair's going to be," Smith said. "It's a good thing I always carry two pair of handcuffs." He laughed and hung up.

MUSIK AND Rodello and Little Johnnie Johnson were done for. The front pages of the newspapers were bursting with news about parole violations. But the crooked parole system wasn't crushed yet. Whoever headed it and fattened off blood and crime wouldn't give up easily.

And two women had seen Smith. They didn't know his name, but they knew what he looked like. And so did Rodello. Word would seep out of prison. The underworld would hear. From now on he would be more hunted than hunter.

And death would be the penalty of error.

NO PAROLE FROM HELL

IN HIS LONE-HANDED FIGHT AGAINST THE VICIOUS PAROLE RACKET WHICH WAS TURNING LOOSE SCORES OF CONVICTED CRIMINALS ON A HELPLESS CITIZENRY, JOHN SMITH HAD SHOWN RELENTLESS COURAGE AND BRILLIANT INGENUITY. BUT HOW COULD HE MATCH A FIENDISH CUNNING THAT TURNED HIS OWN WEAPONS AGAINST HIM—THAT MARKED HIM WITH THE SAME BRAND WHICH HIS ENEMIES BORE WITH BRUTAL AND BLOODY ARROGANCE?

CHAPTER ONE
CRIME PHANTOM

JULY SUNLIGHT poured white and hot on Canal Street. It slashed into narrow Burgandy, Dauphine, Bourbon and all the alley-small lanes of the French Quarter, making the sunny sides unbearable. People strolled slowly, keeping to the shade. It was already too hot to hurry, although the clock at the corner of Canal and Royal streets showed only five after nine.

John Smith parked his roadster on Conti and came down Royal briskly, but without hurry. In starched white cottons he looked as fresh as the July sunlight, and much cooler. He was small, but well built. If you had followed him, watching the easy, athletic stride, you'd have expected a burned, outdoorish face. Instead it was white, whiter than the man's blond hair. It had the sort of whiteness that skin gets from being too long in the dark. There was a pale scar across the white forehead. His eyes were round and marble blue, almost like those of the blind.

On the floor above a Royal Street antique shop was a sign that read:

John Smith
Private Investigator

Smith turned into the doorway underneath.

The police were most upon them....

Jules Le Blanc, who ran the antique shop, was standing there. Smith said, "Good morning, Mr. Le Blanc, good morning. I'll give you even money if the thermometer hits ninety-five today."

Le Blanc backed away, looking frightened. His mouth hung open. He said, "Goo—good morning, Meester Smeth," and vanished into his antique shop.

Smith said, "What the hell?" His private opinion always had been that Jules Le Blanc would die happiest if overtaken by the talking sickness. But this morning the Cajan's one apparent desire had been to get away.

Smith half started to follow and ask what was wrong. Instead he shrugged and went up the stairs to the second floor.

OUTSIDE A door marked *John Smith* he paused, listening. His expression was more puzzled than worried, but his left hand was near his lapel as he twisted the doorknob with his right, pushed, and stepped quickly over the sill.

The room was furnished with a sofa, several chairs, and a desk. Behind the desk sat Bushelmouth Johnson, the huge Negro former prize fighter who now served as assistant and valet for Smith. He lumbered erect, gazing at Smith with an expression somewhat like that with which Le Blanc had greeted the detective.

Beyond Bushelmouth a door marked *Private* stood half open. Bushelmouth said, "Now, Mistur Smiff, you jes'…" but Smith hushed him with a gesture, standing flatfooted, head cocked to one side until his ears, trained during ten years of blindness, told him nothing breathed beyond that open door.

He let his left hand drop to his side. "What the hell's wrong?" he said. "First Le Blanc stares at me like one of us has gone crazy, then I come up here and find you awake. When I didn't hear you snoring I knew something was fishy."

Bushelmouth said elaborately, "Now dat's all right, Mistur Smiff. You jes' set down an' take hit easy. I'se sho glad you actin' natu'l agin."

He followed Smith into the inner office, bringing a pitcher of ice water and a dripping towel. He was grinning, and a person had to look at Bushelmouth twice to believe the vast expanse of white teeth against his face, "You sho musta done some fancy drinkin' since I fix yo' breakfas'. Or maybe hit's de heat cotch you," Bushelmouth said.

Smith said, "Listen here, damnit! What's wrong? What makes you think I'm drunk?"

"I seen you," Bushelmouth said. "Yossur, you sho was flingin' de cutups. You kiss dat gal right out on de street and den you chase Mistur Le Blanc all over his sto' and when I try to grab you, you say you gwine shoot me. Atter you run away, Mistur Le Blanc say you is gone a little daisy in de haid, but Ah knowed you was jes umbriated."

Smith said, "Are you crazy?" But slowly the muscles of his face hardened, bulging his jaws and pulling the cheeks tight. The blue eyes narrowed. "You're sure it was me? It wasn't somebody that looked like me?"

"Aw Mistur Smiff, you know...."

"All right," Smith said. "You *thought* it was me. But it wasn't. I'm not drunk and I'm not crazy. It was somebody that looked like me."

"Yossur," Bushelmouth said, and looked relieved. "But he sho did 'peer lak you."

Smith turned his head to listen, said, "There's a girl coming up the stairs. Get out in the front office."

"You sho can heah pertly," Bushelmouth said, and went into the other office, closing the door.

Crowsfeet etched Smith's temples as he thought over what the Negro had said. Somebody who looked exactly like him had been here a short while ago. And that person had either been, or pretended to be, insane. An almost incredible coincidence—if it was a coincidence. And if it wasn't?

A month ago Smith had undertaken the job of crushing the parole racket in New Orleans and Louisiana. It was a terrific, almost impossible, and dangerous job. Smith had begun it spectacularly. He had attempted to keep his identity secret, because not only the entire underworld but all the political powers of graft and corruption would be out to smash him once he was known. The newspapers had dubbed the mysterious character the Parole Killer, but no one had known his real identity except Claude Vignaux who'd hired him, and Police Lieutenant Rutgers, the one man that Smith could trust. But Smith's last case had landed one man and two women in jail who'd seen him, although they didn't know his name. Rutgers had tried to hold them incommunicado, but there was a chance they'd talked. And if Smith's identity was known, he would be more hunted than hunter. Hunted by men whose very lives depended on his murder.

Thinking of this, Smith heard the steps come up the stairs, turn along the hall and enter the outer office. A minute later when Bushelmouth opened his door he said, "I heard her. She wants to see me about a job. Tell her no."

Bushelmouth said, "Ah 'spected so," and moved to close the door.

Smith heard the girl's shoes tap swiftly, saw Bushelmouth stagger, and then the girl was under the Negro's arm and inside the office.

SMITH STARED at her. In the long years of his blindness he'd forgotten how beautiful a woman can be. Even now the loveliness of this girl was like an electric shock. She had blonde, curly hair, a face like one of Raphael's cherubs, and a body that would make an artist gasp. She said, "Damn it, I'm here and I want to talk to you."

Smith stood up, waving Bushelmouth out of the room. He bowed toward a chair. "Sit down?"

She said, "Thanks," and pulled the chair close to his desk. She sat down, holding a large white leather purse in her lap. For a moment they looked at one another, steady, quiet. The girl said, "You don't look either drunk or crazy now."

"So you saw him too," Smith said. "That wasn't me."

She looked puzzled, then shrugged. "Let it go," she said. "I never believe my eyes anyway." She added, apropos of nothing, "My name's Marion Dark. I've heard of you."

Smith said, "Yes?"

"I've heard that once you blundered in on a bank robbery and one of the bandits slapped you with a bullet." Her eyes were on the pale scar that crossed his forehead.

"You were blind for ten years," the girl went on. "I've heard that during that time you trained your ears to where your hearing was almost unbelievable."

"Not unbelievable," Smith said. "Animals can hear excellently. Most human beings could hear as well as animals if they trained themselves."

"I've been told that during all those years you practiced shooting at sound until you were better than the normal person who sees. And I was told that because your blindness was caused by criminals you came to hate them; that after the operation which gave back your sight you kept on hating them; that you became a private detective because you wanted to strike back."

"You've listened to gossip," Smith said. He was sitting down again, white hands flat on the desk top. "Is that why you want to work with me?"

"Partially." The girl's eyes, so blue they were almost black, looked squarely into his. "I want to work with you," she said slowly, "because you are fighting the parole racket!"

Smith's face did not change, but he could feel the blood rising into it. He tried to keep it down, to keep his eyes empty. "What do you mean, parole racket?"

"Everybody knows who's read a paper in the last month," she said. "You would know even if you hadn't read the papers."

Smith could feel his heart strike heavily at his ribs. Every muscle in his body was rigid. If this girl knew that he was the person who had left corpses of parole violators under the sign "Death Gives No Parole," then other persons would know. And John Smith could hardly expect to live long after the underworld found out.

He kept his voice quiet when he said, "You're on the wrong track, Miss Dark. I'm not that Parole Killer, as the papers call him. I don't want any part of that guy. Business isn't so hot, but it's hot enough without that."

"There's no need to lie to me," she said. "I want to help you, damn it!"

"That's no way for a lady to talk," Smith said. "You look like you belong on mother's knee rather than running around detective agencies anyway."

"I may look that way, but I can shoot straight as most men, and a damn sight straighter. I've worked for O'Rear in New York and for Parkham in Frisco. I've got recommendations from both."

"I'm sorry," Smith said. "I don't have enough work for myself. But thanks for calling."

He first heard the sound as he was standing up. He didn't recognize it then—a soft *click* as though tiny parts of metal had struck together.

"LISTEN," THE girl said desperately. "I know what I'm talking about. And I want to work on the job with you."

"Find the right guy, maybe he'll take you. But I don't want to get mixed up with the matter. I like living too well." He reached to help her from the chair and heard the *click* a second time. This time he knew what it was. The snap of a camera shutter.

He had the leather purse before she knew he was reaching for it. She said, "What…?" and grabbed at it. He shoved her back into the chair, then stepped away, opening the purse.

Inside was a small pearl-handled automatic and a Leika Camera. The camera was sewed to the side of the bag, the lens pointed at the mouth. The purse could be opened a quarter of an inch, pointed at the object wanted, and the shutter clicked with one finger.

The girl did not move while Smith pulled the camera loose and dropped it into his pocket. For a moment he looked at the automatic, hesitating. Then he clicked the purse shut with the gun still inside. He tossed it to her.

"Whom are you working for?" he asked softly. "The politicians and crooks—or the real Parole Killer?"

She looked puzzled. "What do you mean?"

"The crooks might have got me mixed up with this guy in some way and sent you here to make certain. They'd like a picture of the Parole Killer so all their gunmen would know him."

"Yes, but the other…?"

"This Parole Killer, as they call him," Smith said. "He'd like for the crooks to believe it was some other man they wanted. That would turn the heat off him for awhile."

She looked at him squarely. "I'm not working for either," she said. "I want to work for you." She stood up, almost as tall as Smith though she wasn't large.

"Maybe," Smith said. "Maybe. I ought to beat the truth out of you—and I can't. You're too pretty. But whatever you're doing, don't get me mixed in this parole business. Now scram!"

For minutes after she had gone he walked the room. The windows were open against the heat, an electric fan buzzed monotonously, but the sweat on Smith's forehead was cold. He didn't know whether or not he'd fooled the girl. But if she'd suspected his identity then others would also.

All the killers of the city would be after him now, desperate enough to shoot him down on the open street, in his home, anywhere. From now on there would not be one second of safety.

Suddenly he was thinking of the man who'd looked exactly like him, and who pretended to be insane.

CHAPTER TWO
MADMEN SHOOT STRAIGHT

CLAUDE VIGNAUX was a pompous looking man of about sixty. The top of his head was so bald it appeared to have been shaved. Generally he was known as a good but not brilliant machine politician, a member of the parole board, a man who had acquired more money than honor.

The study of his home on St. Charles Avenue was quietly and tastefully furnished. His scotch was excellent and he was one of the few persons who put enough ice in a glass to suit John Smith. Smith took a slow pull from his highball, held the liquor on his tongue to savor the flavor, and swallowed. He kept looking at Vignaux without speaking.

The politician *humphed,* clearing his throat. He always had the manner of a man about to address a political gathering. "I wanted to compliment you on your work in capturing Musik and Johnson and Rodello," he said. "I voted to parole Musik, and after that he gathered his gang and started killing again."

Smith said quietly, "You knew when you voted to parole him?"

Vignaux cleared his throat again, looking embarrassed, but determined. "Yes. I thought he would. I voted because the word came down that Musik had to be paroled. Who wanted him free, who it is that controls the parole racket, I don't know. Maybe the Governor, the Senators, the Representatives don't know. But they take orders because it's political death to do otherwise."

For a moment neither man spoke. Smith knew that Vignaux was thinking of his son. Sam Musik, free on parole, had killed Vignaux's son in a nightclub holdup. Vignaux, who had voted to free the criminal, thought of himself as his own son's murderer. He had sworn revenge, not only on Musik and his gang, but on the entire crooked parole system. He'd hired Smith to carry out that revenge.

Smith swigged at his highball. "Who do you believe heads this racket?" he asked. "You must have some idea."

Vignaux gestured with thick hands. "It's not a local racket," he said. "It's over the country like a plague. I doubt if you can name one notorious criminal who hasn't been released on parole. John Dillinger, Pretty Boy Floyd, Frank Nash. Baby Face Nelson had three paroles. Rube Persful killed five men—and was paroled four times! Read the newspapers. Every day they tell of crimes by paroled convicts.

"Think of what it means to control the parole racket," Vignaux went on. "He can charge a criminal a hundred thousand, two hundred thousand for a parole. Then the crook must murder and rob to get back the money. He can have crimes committed in return for paroles. He has his hand in all the political graft. His power and wealth are limitless. And in every state—"

"I know," Smith said. "But it's the one state we are working on. Who do you think heads the racket here?"

VIGNAUX PACED the room nervously, the ice tinkling in his glass. "I don't know. Dan Snyder, "Boss" Snyder, is supposed to run the politics in this state. But Pete O'Brien, leader of the thirteenth district in the city, is almost as big a figure. But perhaps it's somebody outside them altogether, somebody who controls them. Maybe they don't even know."

"And if I knew the right man?" Smith said.

Vignaux's face was dark with blood. "What good would it do? What proof could convict him? Try and put one of those men in jail! The police are honest, most of them. But crooked politics keeps some men on the force who will do as they are told. There is the gold-plated squad on every force, men with a salary of two or three thousand dollars a year but who have country homes and big automobiles and boats. Boss Snyder could shoot down a man on the street and go free. If the District Attorney prosecuted too well, he'd be out of a job. And if the Boss was convicted, the governor would pardon him."

"That's why I've tried to create as much publicity as possible," Smith said. "It's only the voters who can ultimately correct the system. The editorial pages have complained for years; but nobody reads the editorial pages. I've been putting parole on the front page. Already the public's getting aroused."

Fear showed plainly in Vignaux's face. "I—er—I wanted to mention that," he said. "Do you think, er, so much publicity…?"

Smith finished his highball, said flatly, "It's the only way."

"But whoever backs this," Vignaux said, "he…" His voice got desperate. "Men have been killed for even voting wrong. If it were known that I…."

Smith's white face was emotionless. "Are you getting yellow?" he asked.

"No. No. But—do you think it necessary…?"

Smith stood up. He was a half foot shorter than Vignaux, fifty pounds lighter. "You want me to quit?"

For answer Vignaux took a wallet from his pocket, put ten one hundred dollar bills on the table. "Go ahead," he said slowly. "But for God's sake don't let anybody see you coming here. Don't let anybody know that I…" His heavy face had drained bloodless.

THE CREOLE BAR, on Decatur Street, looked like a dump. The building was squat gray stone, sitting flat against the sidewalk. There was only one pale light outside. The inside was gloomy in the day time and gloomier at night, illuminated by dust-shaded bulbs close to the ceiling. But in the kitchen they gave enough light for the chef to prepare superb oysters and shrimp; and there was enough light for the bartender to always find Smith's favorite scotch. The detective went there frequently.

He turned into the Creole Bar tonight, thinking of the problem ahead. From outside he had noticed there were no strangers. He should have been more careful, but he had only a few months experience behind him and was apt to make mistakes. "If Boss Snyder or Pete O'Brien don't head the parole racket," he was thinking, "at least they should know who does. But how get at them? Approaching them would only land himself in jail, or in the morgue.

He was leaning against the bar before he noticed that anything was wrong. The place was silent, charged with a kind of vibrant and explosive quiet that movement might set thundering. The silence struck at Smith's ears, and all at once he was sweating, cold.

There were no customers in the place except Smith. One bartender stood at the far end of the bar. He was holding his breath, then catching it in deep gulps as he looked at Smith. The other bartender was going out the door, fast.

Smith said, "What the hell, Emile? What's wrong?"

"No theeng, Meester Smeth." The man said the words as though his life depended on it. "Every theeng is all right, yes. You will have a drink?" He began to mix one hurriedly, spilling whiskey. His eyes kept shifting from Smith to a spot near the door. The thing fascinated him. He would look at it and shudder, then at Smith again.

Smith turned, still leaning against the bar. There was a bare spot on the floor, a spot that had been scrubbed not more than a half hour ago.

"Your drink, Meester Smeth." Emile slid it to him, then backed down the bar again.

Smith picked it up. Over the glass he said flatly, "What the hell is wrong around here? What happened to the floor."

Emile looked at the freshly washed spot and shuddered again. "You do not remember?"

"Remember what?"

"You—you—" He got no farther.

Smith heard the sound of running feet on the walk outside. He faced the door, shifting his glass to his right hand, his left coming up close to the lapel of his coat. He shrugged to feel the comforting weight of his gun under his right arm. And all the while he was going backward until he had the end of the bar between him and the door. Emile was in the door to the kitchen, a white-faced chef peering over his shoulder.

The steps pounded to a halt outside, then came on carefully. The door swung open and a uniformed cop came through. He had a police .38 in his right hand. Behind him was the second bartender.

"There he is." The bartender pointed at Smith. He had whispered the words, but in the taut silence they came clear to Smith's ears. "He's crazy as a loon. Be careful."

The cop tried to hide his gun behind him. He spoke as he would have to a small child, but there was a quaver in his voice. "Hello, Budd. How are you now?"

Smith still had the Scotch in his right hand. His left hand rested lightly on his coat. He said, "I'm feeling fine. But I've got an idea there's a mistaken identity around here somewhere."

From the kitchen door Emile said, "He does not remember, no."

THE COP hushed Emile with a stare. He sidled toward Smith as if making friends with a vicious dog. "I'm glad you're feeling all right, Buddy. Why don't you and me have a drink together and then take a ride? It's hot tonight, ain't it?"

Smith said, "Yeah. It's hot." The words came stiffly from his throat. These men thought he was insane. That was obvious enough. And something had happened here recently, something he was supposed to have done. The freshly washed spot near the door seemed to glare at him.

The cop came closer, careful, his gun still behind him. He called, "How about a drink, Emile? Me and the gentleman want a snifter. Ain't that so, Buddy?"

"Sure," Smith said. "Sure." It looked accidental when the drink in his right hand tilted and part of it poured down onto his trousers.

"Oww!" Smith yelled at the top of his lungs. He doubled over, slapping at his leg. "It's acid! It's burning me up!"

Emile said, *"Mon Dieu!* It has him again, yes!"

"I'm burning up!" Smith yelled. He stumbled toward the cop, bent over slapping at his leg. "Help!"

The cop backed away, then stopped, bracing himself. "Here," he said. "I'll help. This'll fix it."

Smith said, "No. This will." He straightened, every muscle in his body behind the left handed swing. Smith was a small man and the cop was a two hundred pounder, but the blow caught him unprepared. It knocked him backward, reeling. He tried to get his gun from behind him. Smith stuck his foot between the policeman's ankle and shoved. The cop went over with a crash. The gun roared and plastering spattered from the ceiling.

Smith poised like a dancer, timing the kick. He couldn't afford to miss. He swung and his toe hit the policeman's wrist. The gun bounced, went skidding against the bar. The cop yelled, rolled, and dived for the gun.

Before he touched it Smith had hit the swinging door with his left shoulder and smashed through. His roadster was parked across the street, but there was no time to get the motor started. He turned to the right, sprinting, whipped down an alley toward the river, then right again.

A block from Canal Street he stopped, crouched at the mouth of an alley until his breathing was normal. Then he turned down the sidewalk, found a drug store with enclosed telephone booths, and went in.

He called headquarters, got Lieutenant Rutgers on the line. "Listen," he said. "There's a mess over at the Creole Bar on Decatur Street. What's wrong over there?"

"What's wrong!" The policeman cursed dully. "Nothing's wrong, John," he said. "Nothing's wrong, except an hour ago you went insane and killed Dave Duncan, one of the cleanest cops we ever had on the force. Shot him in cold blood in the Creole Bar with three witnesses watching you!"

CHAPTER THREE
THE GIRL WITH THE CHERUB FACE

A LONG while Smith heard the words without seeming to understand them. He felt them keep beating at his ears even while Rutgers asked questions and he answered.

"It's the second time today," Smith said over and over. "Twice that somebody who looked like me has pretended to be insane. It's a frameup."

"Maybe." Rutgers' voice was toneless. "Where are you now? I like you, John. I'll do my best for you. But we've got to pull you in."

"It doesn't matter where I am," Smith said. He knew that once in jail he would be railroaded straight to the chair. All the powers of crooked politics would be against him. The honest cops who might believe he had been framed would be taken off the case.

And what chance would he have against the evidence of eye witnesses who believed their own testimony?

He said, "It doesn't matter where I am. I wouldn't be here when you arrived." He forked the receiver and went out.

It was clear enough now. Somehow Rodello, or one of the women in prison who had seen him, had got a description outside. Smith had been identified as the Parole Killer.

Whoever headed the parole racket had been unwilling to have Smith openly murdered. That would have made bigger front page stories than ever, have aroused an already excited public to the point where they would throw out the old politicians and demand cleaner, more efficient government. Smith's murder would have won the very thing he was fighting for.

The man who headed the parole racket had foreseen that, and planned. He had created evidence that Smith was insane. And now if Smith were identified after his death as the Parole Killer, everybody would say, "Why that guy was simply nuts," and all his fight against parole would be discarded. But better than that, he could be shot down as an insane criminal and probably never identified as the Parole Killer. The front page stories would fade away; the public would forget—and the crooked system would continue.

It was up to Smith now, and he didn't have much time. Political bosses would put on the pressure. The word would go out to certain cops on the gold-plated squad to shoot him at sight and claim he had resisted arrest. The man who had planned this wouldn't want to take chances on Smith talking.

The murder had been timed so that Smith had no alibi. It had happened a few minutes after he had left Vignaux's home. The politician might be willing to swear that Smith was in his house at the time, but remembering Vignaux's fright Smith doubted it. He would probably back down in public, claim he had never seen Smith at all. But the head of the parole system wouldn't want to risk that. He had set the stage for Smith's death, and now he would want it swift and sure.

"There'll be men at my home and at the office," Smith thought. "Everywhere they expect me."

The idea stopped him short. His back stiffened, the muscles corded along his jaw. Whoever had planned this frame would be certain to put trusted men at Smith's home and office, men who would carry out his orders to the letter. And those men might be the very ones who could furnish Smith with the information he wanted!

He started swift-legged toward his office.

A BLOCK from it he ducked into a dark doorway and stopped. A street car rattled past, the lights from its windows washing out to both sides of the narrow street. An automobile followed slowly, the street too narrow for it to pass. Squat stone buildings set flush against the walk, most of them dark now. A man and woman passed, wavering slightly, laughing.

Five minutes Smith waited. Then he left Royal, circled to come to the street at the other end of the block beyond his office. Again he waited, using his eyes and ears to search the block.

"They must be waiting inside," he thought.

And then as he was about to step out onto the sidewalk he heard the whistle, very faint and half way down the block. Smith stiffened, fading back into the shadows. From a doorway opposite his office a man appeared. He crossed the street rapidly toward the sound of the whistle, was joined by another man and vanished into the dark doorway of the antique shop under Smith's office.

"So they're waiting there," he thought. Perhaps there were others waiting inside the office, but there was only one way to find out. He stepped back onto Conti Street and started down it rapidly.

There were occasional passersby, but Smith picked out the sound of running steps while they were still half a block away. It was a light, sharp click such as a woman's heels might make. He stepped into a doorway, flattened himself against the wall, left hand close to his lapel, and waited.

The sound of running grew nearer, sharper. Smith let his hand slide under his coat and tighten on his gun butt. His lungs stopped work for a moment, nostrils spread with held breath.

Blonde hair showed in the gloom of the narrow street, and then the girl was past, still running. It was Marion Dark, the girl who had come to his office that morning.

A dozen steps beyond where Smith stood hidden she stopped. He could hear her labored breathing. And then she said aloud, "Damn it! He's got away." The words were muffled because of the way she was panting. "They'll kill him!" she said.

Smith stood there, wondering if she had seen him and was playing a game. There was no sound now except the dull hum of an automobile passing on Royal Street. No one else was in the block.

Suddenly the girl said quite loudly, "John Smith! John Smith! They say you have remarkable ears. I saw you turn the corner a moment ago, and if you are hiding around here listen to me!"

Smith did not move. His left hand still gripped the butt of his revolver.

"Listen," the girl said. "They are waiting in your office. Some cops from the gold-plated squad with orders to murder you. You'll be shot—resisting arrest. There are two of them in your office and two outside on the street. More are at your home."

A woman had turned the corner from Bourbon and was coming toward them. The headlights of an automobile showed a block away. Marion Dark said in a half whisper,

"Good luck, Smith." She walked off, not hurriedly, just someone on an errand.

SMITH WAITED three minutes, then headed for a U-Drive-It company on Dauphine Street. It was only a little after nine when he rolled the Ford out and turned toward the big stores on Canal. They were all closed but there were lights in one shoe store and he rapped on the door until a clerk finally opened up for him.

"We're closed," the clerk said. "I'm sorry."

"I don't want shoes," Smith told him. "I want a ladder."

"A what?"

"One of those ladders you slide around the wall with. I've got a very expensive Persian cat that jumped out of the car near Lee Circle and climbed a tree. I've got to get a ladder quickly and get him down."

"But we don't…." The clerk stopped, gaping at the hundred dollar bill in Smith's hand. It was one of those he had collected from Vignaux earlier.

"That cat's worth a thousand bucks to me," Smith said. "He's won twelve first prizes."

The clerk handled the money like it burned him, but he backed into the store with Smith following. There was only one other clerk still present and it cost Smith another hundred to come out with the ladder. Five minutes later he backed the U-Drive-It into the mouth of the alley that flanked his office, got out and took the ladder with him.

The window of his office was open. Smith crouched underneath in the darkness, listening. There was the drone of an electric fan, the faint mutter of voices, evidently from the outer office.

The back of Smith's neck was goose-fleshed, the hairs stiff as he placed the ladder and started up. Two men were in that office, men with guns out and ready to shoot. Crooks, yes, but still members of the police force, and Smith couldn't afford to shoot them, even in self-defense. Legally he was already a murderer with no right to self-defense.

With his head just beneath the window sill he stopped again. The men spoke in whispers and with long periods of silence between. Three full minutes Smith waited without once hearing Bushelmouth Johnson's voice. "If they've killed him…" Smith thought, and felt a knotting of his throat that had nothing to do with his own fear.

He pulled his gun, keeping his head still below the window. Then, rising and leaning outward, he looked in from the side rather than the bottom of the window.

The back office was empty, the door to the other half open. Through the opening he could see Bushelmouth lying face down near the far wall. Dried blood stained the side of his face and there was a puddle coagulating on the floor beneath him.

To the left of the door he could see one edge of the desk. A man was sitting there, his back to Smith and only one shoulder visible. The other man would be at the left end of the desk. Smith figured, and both would be watching the outer door. There was a coca-cola glass and an half empty bottle of liquor on the desk.

It was difficult getting through the window without breaking the silence that prevailed. Smith had to put his gun back in its holster. Then he pushed down on the sill with both hands, raising himself to where he could get one knee on the window ledge, then both. He twisted sideways, slid his left leg over the window first, balanced on the ball of his foot. Then he got the other leg inside, turning, silent on rubber-soled shoes. The gun was in his hand again as he went toward the door.

ONE OF the men said, "Damn it, Tom, you're getting drunk. Can't you lay off that stuff until we finish here?"

The man who was half visible swayed in his chair and laughed. The first one whispered, "Shut up, you fool! They say that Smith guy can hear a pin drop at forty feet."

Tom said, "What difference does it make? He sure as hell can't hear me before he starts up those stairs. And Nick and Andy are waiting to blast him if he starts down again. He probably won't come here anyway." The man's hand and wrist showed as he reached for the liquor bottle.

Smith went through the door without a sound. His gun was pulled shoulder high, ready for the blow. Taking them by surprise he might get both men without any noise. Anyway, he had to risk it.

And then, as he stepped forward, gun ready, Bushelmouth stirred on the floor and said, "Hotdamn, Mistur Smiff, I'se—"

Their guns had been on the desk in front of them. Both men grabbed and whirled.

"Hold it!" Smith snapped. "Put those guns back on the desk."

For an instant that seemed eternal there was no movement, no sound except the fading echoes of his voice. In that long instant not a man of the four was breathing. Death hung over them, wings spread motionless.

And then Tom hiccoughed drunkenly, said, "To hell with you," and raised his gun.

Smith could have fired three times before the drunk brought his gun level—except that Smith couldn't afford to shoot. These men were cops and he'd never get by with killing a cop sent to arrest him for murder.

He jumped, slapping at Tom's gun with his right hand, swinging his revolver with his left.

Three things happened so close together that Smith could not tell which was first: his right hand touched the other's gun, the gun exploded, his own revolver landed hard on the cop's temple. The man rolled and fell, striking Smith across the waist and knocking him backward.

The second detective had stood motionless before Smith's gun, but now was his chance and he used it. Smith was off balance, the unconscious man lying across his gun arm. Before he could dump him, the other man was raising his gun, almost slowly, carefully. Smith didn't have a chance.

And then Bushelmouth came up from the floor. He came up with his mouth spread in a monstrous, beatific smile, the white expanse of his teeth shining like a rising moon. And with all his two hundred and thirty pounds behind the blow he swung.

His fist cracked flush on the cop's jaw with the effect of an exploding shell. It lifted him, hurled him bodily against the wall. He stood there for a moment as though hooked. Then the hook seemed to pull out and he went down, the body caving in on itself.

Shoes clattered on the stair outside. Men shouted. With one jump Smith reached the door, locked it, snapping orders over his shoulder. "A ladder out the window in the next room! Get those guys out! Hurry!"

"Ah jes as soon us lef 'um heah," Bushelmouth said. But he was carrying the men as he spoke, one in each hand, lifting them by their belts like a couple of suitcases. "Dis gente'mun gwine sho be mad at me when he come to."

"*If* he comes to," Smith said.

Bushelmouth was none too gentle sliding them down the ladder to the alley, and he partially dragged them as he ran along the alley toward the parked Ford.

"Drive," Smith said. "Head for my boathouse on the river." As the car swung into Conti Street shots cracked after them from the office window.

CHAPTER FOUR
BOSS POLITICIAN

THE MEN were still unconscious on the car floor when Smith bound and gagged them. He made a good job of it, using neckties, handkerchiefs, and belts. When he had finished he leaned back, grinning tightly into the darkness.

"I thought you were dead," he said to Bushelmouth. "I saw you lying on the floor with all the blood under you. I thought they'd shot you."

"Nawsur," Bushelmouth said. "When dey come in I was poe-lite and say, 'Mistur Smiff ain't heah but he be heah, Gent'muns.' And dey say, 'We figger he will,' and dey out wid de likker an' de guns."

"It wasn't the liquor put that blood on your head," Smith said.

"Nawsur!" Bushelmouth made a lonesome, dry, smacking sound with his lips. "Ah didn't git me none de likker. But when I seen de guns and hearhd dem say dey was gwine shoot you when you come t'ru de do', I figger I better go tell you 'bout 'em. Den I sta't out and one of 'em knock me down wid his gun, and when Ah goes to git up de odder one knock me down wid his gun, and when Ah goes to git up de nex' time de fust one knock me down again. Well, hit 'peer like I aint gwine git up, so's I jes lays dere."

The car was out of the city now, running fast, the white straight road seeming to rise out of darkness and from under the headlights. Smith was wondering if there was any chance of his boat-house being watched. He doubted it. There weren't more than three or four persons who knew that he had a boat.

Suddenly Bushelmouth said, "Mistur Smiff."

"Yes?" Smith said.

"You 'member what you said?"

"What about?"

" 'Bout when Ah see somebody pint a gun at you an' Ah hit 'em 'fore dey shoot. You 'member?"

"Right," Smith said. "I remember." He leaned forward, pushing a dollar bill over Bushelmouth's shoulder.

The negro said, "Hotdamn! I sho will like me dat Bay St. Louis cawn. Dis legal moufwash…." He spat disgustedly out of the car.

The policemen were conscious when, inside Smith's boathouse, he removed their gags and took pictures of them with the small camera that Marion Dark had used that morning. "There're not many like you boys on the force," Smith said genially. "And the fewer the better. I think I can make some use of these pictures. You boys may find it healthiest to leave town."

The man named Tom was sober now. "What are you going to do?" he asked.

Smith said, "We'll worry about the pictures later. Right now I want to know who sent you boys to my office with orders to be sure I resisted arrest."

"The Lieutenant," Tom said. "Who in hell'd you think?"

"Try again," Smith said. "I want the place the real order came from. Who was it spread the word I wasn't to be brought in alive?"

The cops looked at one another. "We didn't get any such order," Tom said.

Smith sighed heavily. "This is going to hurt me worse than it does you," he said. "But I've got to get at the truth." He pulled his gun and set to work.

A MINUTE later Bushelmouth said, "Hit sho mus' hurt you powerful bad, Mistur Smiff."

Tom broke finally. "All right, damn it," he snarled. "It was Pete O'Brien, the leader of the thirteenth district who told us to gun you. Now what are you going to do to him, huh?"

"I don't know yet," Smith said gently. "We'll find out." He was remembering that Vignaux had named O'Brien as one of the biggest political figures in the state, a man against whom it would be almost impossible to get a conviction on any grounds.

"Was he the guy who ordered me to be framed?" Smith asked.

"What the hell are you talking about? You shot a cop and we were out to get you."

"All right," Smith said. He turned to Bushelmouth. "Let's be going. These gentlemen will be free soon enough."

"And when we do!" the cop snarled.

"When you do. I'd advise you to leave town," Smith said. "The force is better off without men like you on it, so I'm going to turn over your pictures to some stool pigeons of mine. They'll spread them about with word that you are the men who have been fighting the parole system—that you're the Parole Killers. There's a lot of small fry in the underworld who are likely to believe that story, and take some pops at you. You'll probably find Seattle or even Europe a cooler climate. So long, boys."

It was eleven-thirty when Smith made a telephone call from the edge of the city and learned that Pete O'Brien was still at his office. He headed the U-Drive-It toward the thirteenth district.

O'Brien's secretary and general handyman was large and pink-cheeked and blond. He was in his middle thirties, but had been connected with politics in this district for twenty years. He looked up from his desk in O'Brien's outer office as Smith entered. "How-do-you-do-how-do-you-do!" he said. "My name's Heikle, Carl Heikle. Mr. O'Brien's secretary. What can I do for you?"

Smith said, "Tell him John Smith is out here—alive—and wants to see him."

"A strange message," Heikle said. "A strange message, and Mr. O'Brien's busy, but I'll tell him." He stomached across the office to a door marked *Private*. A moment later he was back. "Come right this way, Mr. Smith, right this way."

Smith stepped over the sill, heeling the door shut in Heikle's astonished face. He pulled the chair from in front of O'Brien's desk to where its back was against the wall and it faced O'Brien, both doors, and the window. He sat down calmly, crossing his legs, his left hand toying with the lapel of his coat.

O'BRIEN HAD watched him without moving. He didn't look like the usual Irish politician. He looked more like a very old monkey. He was small and weazened and dark. A mask of wrinkles smothered any expression that might have showed on his face.

For ten seconds the two men faced one another without speaking. Then Smith said deliberately, "I want to know why you framed me for murder."

"Framed you?" O'Brien's voice had a purr. "*I* framed you?"

"Let's not argue," Smith said. "I know damn well you framed me. And then you sent a couple of gold-plated cops to my office with orders to bring back a corpse instead of a prisoner. What I want to know is why."

"All this is news to me," O'Brien purred. "I never heard of you before tonight, Mr. Smith." His wrinkled face might have been that of a mummy for all the expression it showed, but the dark eyes were alive, careful.

There was no sound that normal ears would have caught, but from the outer office Smith heard the whisper of feet. He didn't glance at the door. He kept his eyes on O'Brien's hands. He said, "What was the idea of the frame?"

"You have confused me with someone else," O'Brien said. "I haven't framed you."

For a moment Smith looked worried. He said desperately, "Listen, if you've got me mixed with this Parole Killer the papers have been shouting about, you're wrong. I'm not the man and I don't want to be shot for him."

"What makes you think I'm interested in the Parole Killer?" O'Brien spoke so softly now that most persons would not have heard him.

"Once today I've been accused of being that fellow," Smith said. "A person came to my office this morning and said he had absolute proof I was the Parole Killer. And then tonight, after I was framed, I did some looking around. I looked up this guy who said I was the Parole Killer. He had a couple of photostats of letters."

"Yes?" O'Brien's lips formed the word, but there was no sound.

Smith said, "Yes. I got these photostats. They'd be worth money to the newspapers. I'll turn them back to you, if you take the heat off me."

"How do I know you've got them? What's in them?"

"Plenty," Smith said. They're in my office. That office has a barred door with a bullet-proof peephole. Your cops broke in earlier, but that was when I had only the wooden door closed. I've been back there since, and the inner door, the barred one, is shut now. The window's are bulletproof too. And I've a man in there with orders to let nobody in but me, and not to let me in if there's anybody with me. That's so I won't go back with a couple of your gorillas poking guns in my spine. And if I don't get back at all, tomorrow morning he turns these photostats over to the newspapers."

"And so?"

"So I'll go back there and I'll wait. When headquarters telephones that they've learned I didn't commit that murder. I'll hand the photostats over to you." There was a long minute of silence. O'Brien said, "I don't know what you're talking about."

SMITH STOOD up, his face twisted with anger. "Okay, don't believe me and see where it gets you. If I don't have some word from headquarters by tomorrow night, the pictures go to the papers and to hell with you."

He took two quiet steps, stopping so that the opening door from the outer office would conceal him. He pulled the police special from under his coat. "Call those two bad men that Mr. Heikle has outside," he said gently. "Tell them to come in here—with their hands empty."

For the first time expression showed on O'Brien's face. "Wha—how...?"

"I heard Heikle get them, and who would he be getting but some of your redhots? Call them in."

They came when O'Brien opened the door and called. Smith ducked past them, pulling the door shut. He grinned in the stomachy secretary's face, and was gone.

Bushelmouth was asleep under the wheel. Smith jabbed him hard. "Get going!" he snapped.

They covered one block when he said, "Turn the next corner, slow in that shadow. Go two blocks, then park the car and get the hell away from it. I don't think they'll strike before then. But if you see a car swinging up close, stop this one and scram."

"Yossur," Bushelmouth said. "Dis is sho one busy night, an' me wid eight bits…!"

Smith gave him a five-dollar bill.

"You can't get your liquor yet," he said. "Leave this car, rent another and put it at the mouth of the alley behind my office." As Bushelmouth swung the corner Smith opened the door, dropped off into shadow. A moment later he was sprinting across back yards. Three blocks away he hailed a taxi and was off.…

"Canal and Royal," he said.

CHAPTER FIVE
THE DOOR THAT WAS A MIRROR

THE LADDER was still in the alley beneath Smith's office window. He crawled half way up it and waited until his ears told him no living thing was in the room above. Then he went up and over the sill.

The lock on the outer door had been shot apart, but the door still swung on its hinges. Smith closed it, took the chair in which one of the cops had sat earlier that night, and waited. He could distinctly hear the dull hammering of his heart. His hands were damp with sweat and he wiped them time and again on his handkerchief.

It was a long game he was playing. If he won, the murder heat would be off him and he would be closer to the eventual crushing of the parole system. If he lost…. He knew he would never come to trial on the faked murder charge. "There's no trial—and no parole—for a corpse," he thought.

He had been waiting for eight minutes when he heard steps on the stairway. They mounted steadily, with no attempt at stealth. They had a sound as a man might make in his own home.

John Smith wiped his hands a last time, scrubbing the left one to make sure it was dry. He pulled the gun from its holster, broke it, turned the cylinder, clicked it back again. He stood up, took three long steps and halted close against the door.

The steps were on the landing outside now. They came along the hallway to the door, paused. There was an instant in which the silence was thunderous, in which neither Smith nor the man beyond the door breathed.

John Smith caught the doorknob and pulled. At first he had the impression of gazing into a mirror. The man who faced him might have been an identical twin.

"Come in," Smith said. He had the gun ready in his left hand. "I was waiting for you."

The man who faced Smith did not move, but his nostrils began to widen with a long breath. His mouth twitched. His eyes grew desperate.

Smith did not see the man's hand move. There was only a slight curling of the fingers, a bending of the wrist. But suddenly there was a gun in it, a small derringer fallen from the sleeve. The man fired.

SMITH HAD not seen the hand move, but he had heard the click of the release dropping the gun. The .38 jumped in his hand, its heavy roar drowning the light spat of the derringer. The other man whirled, struck the side of the door, and went down to his knees. The derringer fell lightly to the floor.

Smith heard the detectives shout downstairs and he headed for the back window, lugging the corpse with him. He flung it out the window and went after it, praying silently that Bushelmouth would be at the end of the alley.

He was. "Lawdgod!" he said as Smith reeled up with the corpse. "Hit's two of you. Which of you is you, Mistur Smiff?"

"The live one," Smith snapped. With Bushelmouth's aid he got the body in the car. "Get going!"

"Yossur!" Bushelmouth kicked the starter. The engine caught, sputtered, and stopped.

The wail of the police siren was ear splitting. Smith saw the coupé wheel the corner and head straight for him. From the other direction came one of the gold-plated detectives, firing as he ran.

"For God's sake," Smith said. "Why the hell don't you start that motor?"

Bushelmouth kicked the starter frantically and once more the motor sputtered, half choked, caught again. And then Smith saw that it was too late; the police coupé would be on them before they could get under way.

"Well, I'm whipped," he said.

From the alley across the street a car appeared suddenly, swinging toward the police. There was the wild shriek of brakes as the coupé went into a skid. Bushelmouth said, "Hotdamn! Heah us go!" He swung the U-Drive-It in the other direction and roared away.

A bullet spat through the back window and they were gone. But Smith had caught one glimpse of the driver of the car which had saved his life.

It was the blonde girl who had asked for a job, Marion Dark.

THE FRENCH drip coffee looked black and thick enough to be chewing tobacco. Smith sipped it slowly, reading his paper.

On the front page was the picture of a man sprawled across the doorstep of a very ornate home. Out of the man's chest stood a dagger which served to pin a notice to the body. The notice read:

> CROOKED POLITICIANS PAROLED
> THIS CRIMINAL BUT THEY CAN'T PAROLE
> THE CORPSE

The home, the newspaper said, was that of Pete O'Brien, one of the political powers of the state.

The story told how a man identified as John Smith, a private detective, had been seen to murder a policeman the night before. Police Lieutenant Paul Rutgers knew this was impossible because at the time of the murder the real John Smith was in his office. Later Lieutenant Rutgers had sighted a man identical with Smith in the neighborhood of Pete O'Brien's home. Rutgers had attempted to arrest him, the man had opened fire and been killed by Rutgers. While the Lieutenant was going to a call box to report, the mysterious Parole Killer had carried the body to O'Brien's home and stuck the notice upon it.

Lieutenant Rutgers said, according to the newspaper story, that he believed the bosses of the parole system had attempted to frame Smith because, through some mistake, they had come to believe he was the mythical Parole Killer.

The dead man was a former convict, now out on parole, whose natural resemblance to Smith had been increased by an elaborate makeup. On close observation the makeup was obvious enough, but an excited person would never have noticed it.

"Well," Smith thought, "That takes the honest cops off my trail. I'll get more support from the honest ones now; they'll probably all have a good idea what I'm doing."

But so would the crooks. Last night Smith had bluffed O'Brien. The politician hadn't known whether or not Smith had photostats of incriminating letters, but he was afraid to take the chance. After Smith's description of his office, O'Brien had thought his one chance of getting the letters was to send the man who looked like Smith and let him bluff his way inside. Smith had counted on this to get the man who looked like him into the open. That man was Smith's only proof of his innocence.

He turned the pages of the paper until he found a small inside story telling that two policemen had resigned without previous notice late the night before. Smith grinned.

He was closer to his goal now. He knew that O'Brien was connected with the parole system, whether or not he was the real boss. And he had given the papers another headline story. Everyday now they were carrying front page stories about the abuses of the parole system. Politicians were promising reform at the top of their voices.

"But they won't really do anything unless they are forced to," Smith thought. "I'm a long way from winning."

He wondered if, after this. Lieutenant Rutgers would be able to hold his job, or if O'Brien would put on the pressure to have him removed. It must be obvious to the crooks that Rutgers was covering the Parole Killer; O'Brien would know that Rutgers had lied about Smith being in his office at the time of the murder. The policeman had been glad to cover Smith after he had proof that the private detective was innocent. O'Brien and all the other crooks would want Rutgers off the force, but by helping Smith the lieutenant was getting credit for arrests that made him a great hero, and perhaps the politicians would be afraid to remove him.

"But they won't be afraid to remove me if they get a chance," Smith thought. "And they all know who I am now."

His face tightened with thought. "I'd like to know who that girl is," he said aloud.

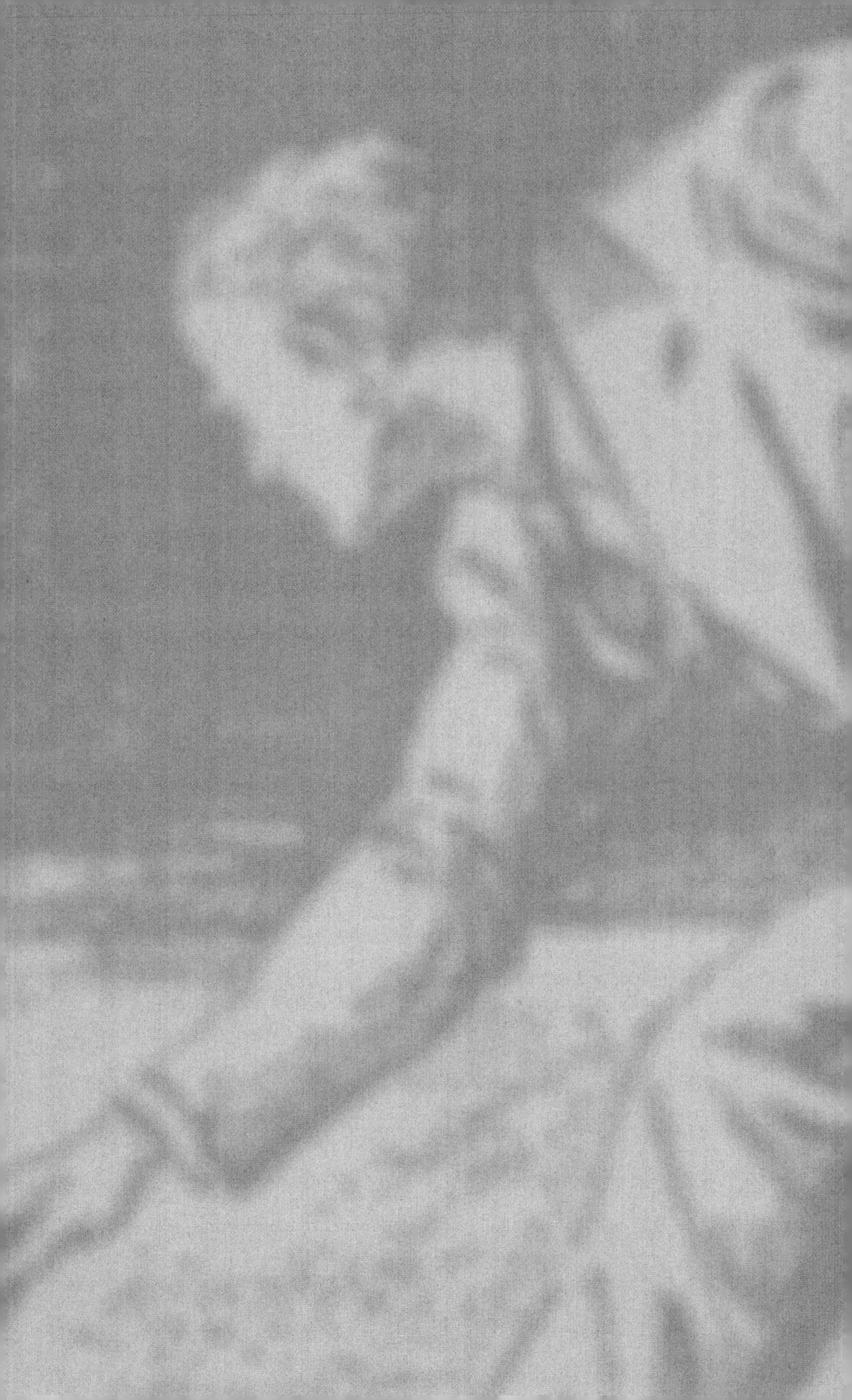

DEATH BREAKS PAROLE

HOW COULD JOHN SMITH, PAROLE FIGHTER, SAVE HIS FRIEND, LIEUTENANT PAUL RUTGERS, FROM THE DEATH THAT GANGDOM HAD PROMISED HIM—WITH ONLY A GOLDEN-HAIRED GIRL TO HELP HIM—A GIRL WHO HAD ONCE SAVED HIS LIFE, AND ONCE ALMOST CAUSED HIS DEATH!

CHAPTER ONE
SPYING ON DEATH

JOHN SMITH crouched by the small upstairs window. His eyes were glued intently on an office building directly across the street—all day he had remained in that position, keeping his lonely watch. And it was a lonely watch—in every sense of the word—for the hand of every political power in the city was turned against him, and the politically-controlled mobsters were out for his life. John Smith had had the nerve to oppose and fight the evilest parole racket that ever blackened a community's name; and in fighting that racket he was attacking the political bosses' most lucrative source of income. Yes, John Smith was very much alone.

As the sun sank lower in the summer sky Carl Heikle came out the door across the street, stomached his way across the sidewalk and stopped by the curb. Hot August sunlight poured over him. With the handkerchief from his pocket he mopped at his pink cheeks and forehead.

Pete O'Brien followed him. O'Brien was the political boss of the 13th District and one of the most powerful figures in the state. He looked like a small, weazened monkey. His face was so wrinkled that no expression could show there. His clothes needed pressing. He and Heikle, his confidential secretary, went off together.

Smith dived headlong for McArthur's gun as the revolver roared.

Smith gazed after them, his face setting in hard, fierce lines. "So that's the guy," he said aloud. "And what am I going to do about it?" The gesture of his small hands showed fury, desperation—and helplessness. His fight against the parole system had bogged down in a blind alley when death closed both ends. He knew that Pete O'Brien was, if not the mysterious figure back of the most foul of all rackets, at least close to that figure. And what could he do about it? Nothing. And throughout the city criminals hunted for John Smith, the "Parole Killer," planning to murder him on sight.

The newspapers said that John Smith, private detective, had left town. Actually, hair and skin dyed to change his appearance, he was living in a small, highly respectable apartment on Prytania, and had rented this room across the street from O'Brien's office in order to keep watch on the politician.

Smith continued his vigil for another half hour, but nothing more happened, and at sundown he was driving out of Prytania in the small, nondescript automobile he'd bought under an assumed name.

He climbed one flight to his apartment, reached for the doorknob and stopped. The muscles of his face were suddenly rigid. His left hand went under his coat lapel, came out holding a police .38. His right hand folded around the doorknob.

Most persons would not have heard the sound beyond the door, the very faint whisper of feet on a thick rug. But Smith had once lived ten years guided by his hearing alone. A bullet from a Parole convict's gun had glanced off his forehead and for a decade he'd been blind before an operation restored his sight. During those years he'd trained his hearing until it was sharp and delicate as that of an animal.

Three full minutes he waited, his ear against the door. Tiny beads of sweat stood on his forehead, colored with the dark powder they had oozed through. Then his nostrils widened in a long breath. He twisted the knob, pitched the door open, and went inside, crouched far over and twisting.

A GIRL was looking out the window across the room. She turned, startled. For a long moment they stared at one another.

Then the girl grinned. "What the hell?" she said. "Do you always come in like that, or is this a special act for my benefit?"

Smith was still crouched, the gun in his hand, and too surprised to move. When he did it was to look toward the rear doorway where Bushelmouth Johnson, the negro who acted as both valet and assistant for Smith, was standing.

"Ah, couldn't stop her, Mistur Smiff," Bushelmouth said. "Dere ain't nothin'! you kin do to dat lady. She jes peers in de doe and she say, 'Heyo, Bushelmouf.' An' I tole her; I say, 'Dis ain't me. Dis is Sam. An' dere ain't no Mistur Smiff live heah nether so tain't no need to ask fer him.' Dat's what I tole her, Mistur Smiff, but she wouldn't pay me no heed."

The girl was still grinning. "It's not Bushelmouth's fault, really. Or maybe it is. I was lucky enough to see him on the street this morning and trailed him here."

Smith had straightened slowly. He put the gun back in its holster, closed the door behind him. "I was a fool for letting Bushelmouth go after groceries," he said, and waved the negro out of the room. He was thinking that if Marion Dark had found him then someone else might have also. And discovery for Smith meant death.

The girl had a face like a cherub, with soft gold hair curling close to her head and very wide and innocent eyes. Smith had met her once before and whenever she cursed, which she did mildly but frequently, the words came as a distinct shock.

Now she said, "You're a hell of a host. Don't I get to sit down? Don't I get a drink or some hospitality around here?"

"**YOU GET** both," Smith said, and gestured toward a chair while he yelled for Bushelmouth to make a couple of highballs. "I'd like to thank you," he said. "The last glimpse I had of you, you were driving out of an alley in the Vieux Carre. Perhaps it was coincidence, but you came at the exact moment to head off another car and save my life. And a little while before that you'd been trying to take a picture that would get me killed. Which side are you working for?"

"I told you I wanted to work for you. I told you I wanted to fight the parole system."

Smith swallowed, muscles standing out in his neck. "But I—"

"Isn't it too late to keep up that pretense?" she asked. "Every crook in town, and that includes the politicians, knows who the Parole Killer is."

The ice tinkled in Smith's glass. Over the rim he watched her. "You look as if you had wings, or should have," he said. "You look as if you belong on mother's knee. And you want to get a job that's almost sure death."

"You don't look so damn tough yourself," she said, "even with that mustache. And that blond hair dyed black. You look like a dude."

She stood up sharply. There was a vibrant tenseness about her that clashed with the softness of her face. "I came to tell you about Lieutenant Paul Rutgers," she said. "Maybe you'd like to know that the politicians are kicking him out."

"What!" The round, marble blue eyes seemed to freeze, the face to grow stiff.

"A few months from now he'll be off the force with no pension and no way to make a living—unless some crook has 'accidentally' killed him."

Smith was standing now. He was a small man, scarcely taller than the girl before him, but well made. "They can't do that," he said huskily. "The newspapers are playing Rutgers for a hero. The public won't—"

Without Rutgers on the police force to help him there'd be no chance of finishing his fight against the crooked parole system. Without Rutgers to cover him the first time, Smith was forced to kill a criminal in self-defense. He would have the police as well as the underworld after him, politics would railroad him through a crooked trial straight to the chair. And Smith liked the little, desperately honest policeman. Now Rutgers was going to lose his job, his future, perhaps his life because he'd helped John Smith fight the parole racket.

Smith was thinking suddenly of the ten years of darkness, of never knowing if he'd see again—years caused by a paroled convict's return to crime. That was his personal score against a foul system, but there was more than that. He knew that almost every famous criminal had been paroled. Dillinger, Pretty Boy Floyd. Baby Face Nelson killed three G-men after his *third* parole. Every G-Man ever killed on duty was murdered by a paroled convict. Parole—a crooked system run by crooked politicians who fattened on theft and murder.

"Don't underestimate the man you're against," Marion Dark said. "He couldn't afford openly to kick a hero off the force. But you saw in the morning paper about the two gamblers murdered out on the edge of town?"

"Yes."

"Rutgers is going to be sent to solve that. Only he'll have a desk job so he can't do any real work. And the politicians will make sure that the crookedest cops on the force are the ones he has under him."

"But the cops," Smith said desperately. "They're—"

"Sure. Most of them are honest. But the politicians keep a few diamond studded boys on the force. Those are the ones Rutgers will have. He'll stay out there where he can't help you until the public has forgotten him. They forget quick. And then he'll be kicked off altogether."

"The public—" Smith said and stopped. It was only the public who could actually win the fight on parole. Only the public could throw out the old, crooked politicians and demand honest government. But the public didn't realize how rotten the system was. That was why Smith had used tactics which made parole a front page story. And the public was becoming aroused. The crooked political bosses were frightened. They had determined to get Smith and every man who helped him.

SMITH CROSSED the room, hands clenched hard. "If Rutgers caught those killers—" he said.

"Caught—hell. Ryan Hardick and Nick Tomelli did the job. But they are Pete O'Brien's boys; what can Rutgers do? If he had any proof, O'Brien would give the order and somewhere the proof would vanish. If he had any witnesses they'd either vanish, or forget. O'Brien had those guys killed because they weren't paying tribute for their gambling house—and so he'd have a reason to send Rutgers so far in the country there won't be anything he can do but grow tomatoes."

Smith's face got fury-white. Red veins came in his eyes. His mouth set hard and ugly. What the girl said could be true. O'Brien was nominally leader of only the 13th district, but his power was statewide. There wasn't a chance of convicting a man O'Brien sponsored. The prosecuting attorney and the judge would have their orders; even the Governor, if it camel to that. Murder made safe by politics.

"Listen," Smith said after a moment. "How do you know all this?"

"How does any detective learn things? Stool pigeons. Pipe lines. You want to hire me?"

He didn't answer. His highball glass was empty now, but he still held it, fingernails whitened from pressure. "This Ryan Hardick and Nick Tomelli you claim did the shooting—what proof have you got?"

"None. There weren't any witnesses."

"And what proof would convict them?"

He knew the answer before she said, "None, with O'Brien passing out orders and money."

He crossed the room twice, noiseless on the thick rug. "What do these guys look like?"

She said, "I thought you might want to know. Here's a couple of pictures the state made of them once, before they had O'Brien's backing. They are out on parole now."

She held out two regular prison photographs, front and profile. Smith looked at them, then at the girl. "This fellow—"

"Hardick," she said.

"This Hardick, he's superstitious?"

"He kills because he likes it," Marion Dark said. "But a black cat stands his hair on end. He goes to church twice a week. He enjoys knocking off other people, but he wants to avoid his turn, and at least to be ready when it comes."

"I've seen those two gentlemen," Smith said. "They came out of O'Brien's office today, twice. And both times they stopped and put on a kind of act."

"You can't use that for proof."

"Maybe," he said. But he had to use something for proof. Here was his one chance to carry on the fight. If he could break this case it would put him closer to the head of the parole system, it would save Paul Rutgers, and it would add more fire to the growing public indignation. But how break it when it was admitted that nothing could convict one of Pete O'Brien's boys? Murder had been made safe, by politics.

It was five minutes after the girl left that the phone rang. Lieut. Rutgers corroborated everything she had said.

CHAPTER TWO
SWAMP DEATH

NEXT TO the building housing Pete O'Brien's office was a small furniture store. Smith was studying the window display when the men came onto the sidewalk, but the mirror of a dresser in the window allowed him to watch them. One was small and plump, the other dark with bushy brows. Ryan Hardick and Nick Tomelli.

It was eleven o'clock in the morning. Traffic rattled along the street and a block away a streetcar made a grinding rumble, but Smith, straining his ears, could hear what the men said.

Tomelli, the dark fellow, grabbed Hardick by the arm, said, "Have you got it?"

"I thought you had it," Hardick said. He looked frightened and dug through his pockets.

"Me? Why, damn you, I..." The bushybrowed man wet his lips as though he were afraid. He plunged his hands into his pockets.

"It musta been left," Hardick said. "We gotta get it!"

"If the cops found it..." Tomelli looked sick. "Jesus! I don't wanta burn!"

"Let's go!" Hardick said. "Hurry!" They started down the walk.

Smith kept looking in the store window as they passed directly behind him. There was something crazy here, something that he didn't understand.

What he'd heard sounded as though somewhere they'd left vital evidence on the gambling house murders.

"I think I'd better investigate," Smith said to himself. He turned away from the window, walking carelessly but fast.

Hardick and Tomelli were a half block away near their parked car. Tomelli, meaning to circle to the drivers seat, swerved so that he passed on one side of a telephone pole while Hardick was on the other. The plump man stopped short, cut back so as to go on the same side of the pole with Tomelli. Smith could see him muttering and Tomelli cursing at him. That guy was superstitious all right.

Smith's car was parked not far from theirs. He swung out into traffic behind them and took up the trail. Hardick drove fast, but kept inside the traffic laws and it wasn't hard to tail him. Evidently he was more worried about getting where he was going than about being followed.

At first Smith thought they were going directly to the gambling house where the murder had been committed, but a few blocks away they stopped. Tomelli made a telephone call before Smith could park, then came back to the car again. Smith tailed after them, out through the suburb, about ten miles along the Mobile highway, then onto a shell road cutting back into the bayous.

Here he let the car ahead get out of sight. He didn't want them to know he was following and this was a desolate road with few crossings. It would be comparatively easy to trail them.

BUT THERE was something fishy about this whole business, he thought. He couldn't get over these men going through the same actions, perhaps even saying the same words, three times in two days. It didn't make sense.

And what could they have left out on this lonely road? In places it was scarcely wide enough for two automobiles to pass. Black bayou water bordered it on each side, thick with lilypads, and beyond the strip of water was impenetrable swamp. Cypresses held their lace-worked leaves high into the sunlight. Below them were the gaunt skeletons of oaks wrapped in drooling moss. Underneath the moss it was almost twilight-dark, dark water and muck, underbrush, dead logs rising out of the slime. Once Smith saw a moccasin slithering off into the water as the sedan approached.

And then, in his rearview mirror, he saw the car following him. A sudden chill went along his spine. His mouth got dry. He put his left hand under his coat and loosened the .38 in its holster. His eyes left the road for a moment, staring out into the swamp.

The road twisted through trees. Shells whirred under his tires as he went into the curve. His right hand was very tight on the wheel, his left hand barely touching it but tense and ready to jerk upward at any instant. It was almost as though he had known he would turn the bend and see the road ahead blocked by the car he had been following.

There was the sputter and roar of machine gun fire. Flame lashed at him from the car that was pulled sideways across the road and parked. Holes pricked through his windshield and then the whole thing was gone in a mass of flying glass. He felt no pain but all at once blood was flowing down his cheek.

The .38 special was in his left hand. He fired three times, carefully but fast. Not more than twenty yards separated the cars and he saw the spiderwebbing on the glass windows where his bullets struck. The car ahead was bullet-proofed!

From behind came another blast of machine gun fire as the second car came up. His back window blew out. Bullets ripped into the car body.

Actually Smith had been moving, sliding down for protection between the seat and the dash, with that first sight of the machine ahead. His own car never stopped, the whole thing lasted less than five seconds, but he had the impression of infinite time, of thoughts plodding slowly, one after another, through his head.

It was a trap, arranged from the first. And it was the girl who had put him on the trail of Hardick and Tomelli! Once before she tried something which might have resulted in his death. And once she had saved his life. But this time would be the end.

Smith was on his knees, one eye cocked above the dash. He held the steering wheel with his right hand crossed under his left arm. The left hand held the .38. He picked out the narrow slit through which the machine gun was blasting, steadied his revolver.

The car lurched wildly as he fired. He knew that his front tires were gone. The sedan was slowing down despite his knee on the accelerator. One of the back tires was shot, and flung shells made as much noise as the machine guns. Bullets whanged into the steel body, dug through or went screaming out into the swamp.

HE DIDN'T have a chance and he knew it. He couldn't even drive fast enough to wreck the car ahead and die with the satisfaction of knowing that he took two criminals with him. He couldn't circle the car and he couldn't back up because of the one behind. They had him.

And then he thought of the water bordering the road. He didn't know how deep it was, but he had to risk it. He kept his knee on the accelerator, pushed the brake with his left hand, jerked the steering wheel with his right. The car went into a wild skid. It turned completely around. It teetered at the road's edge. It plunged it over sideways.

What happened in the next few seconds Smith couldn't say. He felt his body slammed back and forth. His head hit the dash and new blood flowed over his face. His gun was gone. His leg was tangled between the brake and the clutch and felt as though it were broken. Water closed over him.

He knew that if he got free of the car they would kill him. Even if he swam under water to the edge of the swamp they would see him there and shoot him down. He struggled, felt one hand rise above the surface. Then his head was up and he was gulping dark air.

He'd managed to turn the car completely over so that it sank with the wheels up. The water was only about five feet deep and now there was a small pocket of air close to what had been the floor of the automobile. There wasn't room to get his whole head out of the water. He had to keep his neck bent sideways, but he could breathe.

He heard men calling to one another, the crunch of shell under leather. Tomelli said, "Well, that's that."

"It wasn't no fun," Hardick's voice complained. "We didn't even get a look at the guy."

A strange voice, one of the men from the rear automobile probably, said, "Oh, it was him. After you telephoned we drove right past him once. He'd dyed his hair, but it was Smith all right."

It was getting hard to breathe in the narrow space between water and car. The air was thin and hurt his lungs. He tried to breathe slowly, to hold the air as long as possible.

And then he heard Tomelli's thick voice saying, "There may be a little air left under that car. The guy could still be alive."

Hardick said, "Like hell he is. I musta cut him apart with the tommy."

"But there's a little space," Tomelli said again.

One of the men from the back car said, "The boss is gonna give us hell if we don't get the body outa there. You know how he kept saying to fix the stiff so nobody would find it."

"How the hell you gonna get it?" Hardick asked.

"We got to find a wrecker," the other man said. "We *got* to get that body!"

"Won't nobody come along this road. We got time. Let's go."

"But there's a little air under there," Tomelli said again.

ONE OF the men said, "Oh hell, you can fix that if you're worried. There's gas all over the water. Throw a match on it. If the guy's alive he'll cook."

John Smith thought he was going to be sick. Such a terror as he had never known crawled cold and slimy through his veins. His chest hurt and there was a dull roaring inside his head that seemed to repeat over and over, "If the guy's alive he'll cook."

"I'd rather be shot," he thought. He couldn't crouch there in the dark and roast like a trapped rat. He would dive, either drown trying to get out of the car or come up to the surface and be killed with a blast of machine gun bullets. It was better that way. He took a breath of the hot thin air.

It struck like a blow on the back of the neck. It jolted him, knocked his head forward, knocked the air out of him. He couldn't believe the sound until it came again—the wild shriek of a police siren! A sudden burst of gunfire!

One of the men in the road said, "For God's sake, what...?"

"Let's scram!"

There was the noise of running. Then Tomelli's voice, "But suppose the guy's alive? There's air...."

Hardick answered from up the road. "You stay and chuck a match on him." Car motors burst into life. Smith heard Tomelli running along the shell road. He didn't know whether or not the gunman had dropped the match which would burn him. Both cars roared off.

He couldn't wait for the sound of fire. The oxygen was gone from the small air pocket underneath the car. He had to dive, try to get free even if he came up into a hot, searing sheet of flame....

CHAPTER THREE
BAY SAINT LOUIS CORN

SMITH'S HEAD broke the surface and he gulped air into bursting lungs. The water lilies tugged at him, threatened to pull him down again. He floundered about, saw that no wave of fire rolled at him and for moments he was too relieved to see anything else. He beat his way through the lily pads and crawled onto the shell road.

He stood there panting for moments before he remembered the police siren and the gunfire which had saved him. But now the road stretched pale and empty to right and left until it curved and the dark swamp walled it in.

Far off to the right was the fading sound of automobiles. That would be the two cars with the gunmen. He was certain that no other machines had passed, but when the sound of those cars was gone there was only the faint whisper of the wind against the cypresses, the sleepy lagging chirp of a cricket, the drip-drip of water dropping from his clothes to the road.

What had happened to the police car? He couldn't figure it out. He started walking back down the road toward the city. He took three steps—and stopped.

Somebody beyond the curve was walking toward him!

Instinctively his left hand came up toward his shoulder holster before he remembered it was empty. There wasn't any place to hide so he just waited. The crunch of the shoes got louder and then Marion Dark came around the curve.

For a half minute they stood and looked at one another. The cherub face was puckered with fear and grief that kept the facial muscles stiff even after the emotions were gone. And then she said, wonderingly, "I was afraid—you're not dead?"

"Not yet," Smith said. "You put the finger on me all right, but your trigger men didn't do a clean job."

She kept staring at him. "I don't understand," she said. "I didn't…."

"You didn't put me on the trail of these guys, knowing they were laying for me all the time?"

She said, "You damned fool. I told you they killed those gamblers. They did. But I didn't tell you to go up and introduce yourself to them, then come out where they could kill you without interruption."

Smith's round blue eyes studied the girl and she looked back at him steadily. If she was telling the truth, how had this trap been planned ahead of time? How had Hardick and Tomelli know he would trail them?

And then he thought about their strange actions outside the office doorway. Suppose O'Brien, or whoever was the power behind him, had figured that Smith, knowing O'Brien to be connected with the parole racket, would watch O'Brien's office? And suppose he had known that Smith would learn of Hardick's and Tomelli's connection with the gambling murder, had allowed Rutgers to learn that much so he would tell Smith. Knowing that, O'Brien could be almost certain that Smith would follow the killers if he overheard their remarks about leaving evidence. Then Tomelli had made his phone call, and the trap, already planned, was set.

THEY HAD not wanted to murder Smith openly because of the way the public, already aroused over the parole racket, would howl. Smith's death might gain the very thing he fought for in life: indignant citizens voting out the old, graft-corrupted politicians, demanding honesty from their officials. So O'Brien, or the shadowy figure back of him, if there was one, had wanted Smith simply to disappear. "The boss is gonna give us hell if we don't get the body outa there," one of the gunmen had said. "You know how he kept saying to fix the stiff so nobody could find it." With Smith's disappearance the fight against the crooked parole system would simply fade from the front pages. The public would forget. The old system would continue.

"It could have been that way," Smith thought. "Maybe that guy's smarter than I've been willing to admit." And it could have been the girl.

"If you didn't put the finger on me," Smith asked, "how did you happen to be here?"

"A hell of a guy you are!" she said angrily. "I wish they had killed you!" She turned and went swiftly back down the road.

Smith stared, then he was loping around the curve to catch up with her. He walked beside her toward her parked car. "I'm sorry," he said. "I didn't want to make you angry. But I—can't trust anybody in this job. I've got to be careful." He was angry at himself for apologizing, angry because he wanted to. And yet he did want to. He wanted to explain, to say he hadn't meant to hurt her.

She turned to look at him and he was surprised at the misty sheen of her eyes. But she was grinning again. "I come out and save your life," she said, "and what kind of thanks do I get?"

"*You* saved my life? You mean...."

"You were tailing Hardick and Tomelli and I was tailing you. When that car full of apes cut in behind you on this road I knew what was coming. There wasn't time to get the police The shooting started while I was trying to make up my mind what to do. So I used my siren and backfired the car trying to bluff them away. I didn't really think I was doing any good. I thought you were dead."

Smith's wet hands made dark spots on her shoulders as he turned her to face him. "If they'd caught you—" he said huskily, and didn't finish. "You took that chance...."

The girl laughed, a little nervously. "I didn't take any chance—not for a sawed-off private cop. I was careful to turn my car around first. I'd have been half way back to New Orleans before those guys could have reached the curve." They were driving along the shell road when Smith asked, "What was the idea of tailing me? Who are you working for anyway?"

She glanced at him, then her blue gaze went back to the road. "I came along for the fun," she said. "But I'd like to work for you."

"Why don't you try the truth sometimes?"

She hesitated. Then said, "I told you the truth."

"Maybe," Smith said. He wanted desperately to know. If she were honest, she could help him. If she was lined up with the crooks and he trusted her it meant death.

"**AH DON'** know as I feels right 'bout us bein' heah," Bushelmouth said. "Hit's housebreakin', Mistur Smiff."

"Shut up," Smith said.

"Yassur. But hit don' seem right to come bussin' in dat nice young lady's 'partment an' she ain't eben heah to say 'come in' er 'git out'."

"Shut up," Smith said.

"Yassur. How come you think she gwine come floozyin' in heah wid a couple dem cemetery-fillers? She don' look to me lak the kinda gal would have no tripe wid such folks. I don' bleav she do it."

Smith said, "Shut up."

"Yassur. But Ah—" He looked at Smith's face and became quiet.

"They're coming," Smith said softly. His lips were hard and thin. His eyes pulled Bushelmouth after him as he backed out of the living room into the rear of the apartment. "Do exactly what I told you," he said, and grated the words through clenched teeth.

A moment later the hall door opened. Smith heard Marion Dark say, "Sit down, boys. Take it off your feet." Then she called, "Ethel! Come on out. We've got company."

Bushelmouth answered, "He say to say she say she ain't heah right now on account she gone to de drugsto' fer a minute and she be right back, but dat—" Smith's hand landed hard over the negro's mouth. It didn't cover the vast expanse of shining teeth, but it stopped the words.

In the next room the voice of Nick Tomelli broke sharp, nervous. "Who the hell's that? What did he mean?"

Marion giggled. "That's Sam, the negro who cleans up for us. He's not very smart." She called, "Make us three drinks, Sam."

Smith kept his hand pushed on Bushelmouth's lips although he had to reach high to do it. He called, "Yes'um," then said in a tight whisper that only Bushelmouth could hear, "You use your hands when the time comes. And keep your damn mouth shut."

"Yassur," Bushelmouth said. "But—" The look in Smith's eyes stopped him.

Smith mixed the drinks himself, handed them to Bushelmouth. The negro started to say something, caught Smith's gaze, choked on the words. Muttering to himself and shaking his head, he took the tray into the front room.

THERE WAS a long-barreled revolver in Smith's left hand as he watched through the cracked doorway. Hardick and Tomelli were on a sofa to her right, Marion between them. The plump man had his arm around the girl and her gold hair cradled on his shoulder. But Tomelli sat bolt upright. His bushy brows were pulled into one continuous line across his forehead. He looked nervous. When Bushelmouth handed him a drink he smelled it, tasted carefully.

"Here's to a pleasant evening," Marion said. "Success to the plans on foot."

"You must be reading my mind, baby," Hardick said. "I'm glad you feel that way about it." He lit Marion's cigarette, his own, then jerked the match away as Tomelli reached for it.

"Three on one match," he said. "You're crazy."

Bushelmouth had circled the sofa and come up behind it. He stood for a moment gazing down at the men, a puzzled look on his broad face. "Why in hell doesn't he go ahead and conk them?" Smith wondered. He tried to hurl his thoughts at the negro, "Go ahead! Go ahead!" Tomelli was getting nervous.

Bushelmouth raised a fist that looked like a head of a nine pound hammer. There was a sort of wistful expression on his face. He balanced carefully. He brought the fist down on the top of Hardick's head.

The plump man's whole body went down as though it had been driven into the sofa. His head seemed to vanish into his shoulders. He stayed that way a moment, then the springs of the sofa raised him gently. He swayed and was crumpling when the girl put her arm around him.

Bushelmouth had stepped to the edge of the sofa beside Tomelli, but made no motion to hit the gunman. Tomelli had been dazed for only a second, not understanding what had happened. Then like an uncoiling spring he came upright. His hand flashed under his coat and out. There was the gleam of light on blue steel.

A groan caught in Smith's throat as he plunged through the doorway. He cried hoarsely, "Hit him, you fool!" His own gun was raised shoulder high to strike but he saw that he couldn't make it. He jerked it down, finger tightening on the trigger!

But he had figured without Bushelmouth. The negro waited until Tomelli's gun was free of his coat—and then he swung. The blow had the free flowing motion that once had made Bushelmouth Johnson a top flight heavyweight. It had all his two hundred and thirty pounds behind it. It landed flush on Tomelli's jaw.

The Italian seemed to leap into the air and backward. When his feet touched the floor he skidded as though he were on roller skates until he hit the wall. It bounced him forward and he went down hard on his face.

Smith had pulled to a stop, panting. "Bushelmouth," he said a little plaintively, "why in God's name did you wait so long to hit him?"

Bushelmouth shifted his great feet and looked embarrassed. "Well, Mustur Smiff, Ah—well, you know.... He had de gun out befo' ah hit him."

Marion was still on the sofa cradling Hardick against her shoulder, "He damn sure did," she said.

"Well, you didn't say nothin' 'bout hittin' folks widout no guns, Mistur Smiff. But you 'member one time...."

Smith sighed and said, "Oh, my God." From his pocket he took a dollar bill and handed it to Bushelmouth. "Okay," he said. "Go on out and get it."

"What's all this?" Marion asked.

"Bay St. Louis corn whiskey," Smith said. "Bushelmouth doesn't like the legal stuff."

"Hit tase lak ole coffee mix with dishwater," Bushelmouth said. "Hit ain't got no mule."

"I told him that if ever he saw anybody pull a gun on me and he hit the guy before he could shoot, I'd give him a dollar for corn whiskey. So now, after I figure out a method to get these guys without making any noise and having the neighbors call the cops, Bushelmouth stands there waiting for the man to get his gun out so he can make a dollar. I didn't put any Micky Finns in that liquor because I was afraid to risk them noticing you pick a certain glass, and anyway there would have been several seconds during which they'd have known they were doped before they passed out. They might have started shooting, so I sent

Bushelmouth out to conk them from the back." He shook his head wearily, then set about tying up the men. They would be out for minutes yet.

"I still don't know why you asked me to bring these boys up here," Marion said. "Even if you beat a confession out of them, make them sign it, you wouldn't get anywhere. Not against Pete O'Brien."

"I want these boys to write out their own confessions," Smith said. "I want 'em to include the man who hired them for the job. Maybe then I can make a trade."

"They'll never do that. You're crazy."

CHAPTER FOUR
POLITICS CAN'T HELP YOU IN HELL

"MAYBE IT won't work," Smith said. "But I've an idea, and I can't be any worse off." He told Bushelmouth to lug Tomelli into one of the bedrooms and gag him. Then he waited until Hardick, propped upright on the sofa, regained consciousness.

"Okay," Smith said then. "We can get down to business now. I want a written confession to those gambling murders, Mr. Hardick. The exact time you and Tomelli went there, all the details, how much you were paid for the killing and who paid you."

Hardick stared back at Smith. He was a rather innocent looking man at first glance, but now Smith could see in his eyes the thing which made him a killer. "You can go to hell," Hardick said softly.

"I don't want to have to beat you to death," Smith said, "But I will if necessary."

"You can go to hell," Hardick said again. He sat very still, like a rock.

Smith worked on him a little with the barrel of his gun. He didn't expect to get anywhere this way. This was bluff, buildup for what was to come later. "Listen," Smith said. "I don't mind killing you if I have to. Had you rather go out this way or take a good long prison term?"

"I don't know anything about those killings," Hardick said. "If I did and if I talked, I wouldn't get any prison term. I'd rather bump off this way."

That was how O'Brien kept his boys in line, Smith thought. He'd read of gangland killings, victims horribly butchered and tortured. Any death was preferable to what a squealer would get, so the boys kept quiet.

"Okay," Smith said. "If you think this is going to be easy, I'll try a different method."

Marion Dark had watched from an overstuffed chair, sipping a drink. She looked frightened now. "You mean you're going to try—that thing?"

"I am," Smith said, and went out of the room, leaving his gun on the table. Marion got up and backed to the far corner. "For God's sake, be careful," she called. "It might kill all of us."

Smith came back wearing heavy leather gloves. With both hands he gripped a black and green snake just behind the head. He walked over close to Hardick, the snake's tail coiling around his arm.

The gunman was a sick yellow. His eyes bulged out of his head. "What—what are you going to do?"

"Have you ever heard of the Green Mamba of Africa?" Smith asked. "Next to the King Cobra it's the most deadly snake in the world. It doesn't kill as fast as some, but there's absolutely no antitoxin for its bite. You swell up about four times your normal size and you turn purple and die."

"Wha—what—" The words were too thick for Hardick's throat. His skin was a mottled yellow and green. The muscles of his neck worked. "You—you wouldn't—couldn't kill—"

Smith pushed the snake closer. "Somebody's killed a lot of crooks lately," he said. "Pinned signs about parole on their chests with knife blades. You're on parole, aren't you?"

"I—I…." Saliva spilled over the man's chin. His popped eyes were bloodshot.

"If you don't believe I'll kill you," Smith said, "Just keep quiet for five seconds." He began to count.

"All right," Hardick whimpered. "I killed 'em. Me and Tomelli shot 'em. Wes were running another gambling house in the same district and…."

The snake was less than half an inch from Hardick's eyes. "You're lying," Smith said. "Who paid you for killing them and how much?"

"Nobody paid. I—"

"**TO HELL** with you," Smith said. He made a gesture as though to push the snake forward, then tried to pull it back. Hardick screamed. At the same instant, Marion, who had come close behind Smith, stumbled. She hit his arm, knocking it forward. The snake struck just above Hardick's eye.

The man went mad, more from fear than from pain. Smith had to gag him momentarily. He writhed, chewed at the gag, froth spilling from under it. Finally, exhausted, he lay still and Smith removed the gag. "Get me a priest," Hardick begged. He was whimpering, sobbing like a baby. "I got to be ready before I die."

"I'll get you the priest," Smith said, "—if you write out a confession for me first."

"Get the priest!" Hardick cried. "I'm dying!" His face was already swollen and; turning purple.

Smith untied one arm for him, gave him paper and pen. "Write it all out," he said. "Who paid you the money, everything."

Hardick yelled, "No! Not to you. Get—"

"I'm not calling anybody until you write it for me," Smith said. He thrust his face close to Hardick's. His voice shook with tension. "You'll be going to hell in an hour and Pete O'Brien and all his politics can't help you then! He's the man who's sending you there. Are you going to die with that on your soul? Are your last words going to be a lie about murder you've committed?"

"All right!" Hardick sobbed. "All right!" He grabbed the pen and wrote.

When he finished. Smith said, "Okay, pal. You'll have plenty of time for anything you want. That was a black snake with green paint on it. They hurt worse than a bumblebee, but they're not much more deadly. I've watched how seriously you dodge bad luck. I thought you'd be serious about the last thing you ever did."

Hardick stared at him. He was still panting, sobbing. Along with his panting he began to curse, steadily. "You'll embarrass the lady," Smith said, and gagged him again.

It was easy after that. He brought in Tomelli, showed him the confession and got another one. Both stated that Ross McArthur had paid them a thousand dollars for the murders. McArthur was nominally leader of the district in which the killings had taken place, but most persons knew that he took O'Brien's orders.

"Well, you've got that much," said the girl. "But what have you got? I told you that a confession wouldn't convict one of O'Brien's boys. Something will happen to those two before they reach the court room. Or the judge will find a flaw. Or the jury'll be bribed."

"Maybe," Smith said. "But at least it's going to put McArthur in mighty hot water. The publicity will force him out of his job. And if we can get a conviction on these boys, then McArthur would talk to save his own hide. And then we'd have O'Brien."

There had been noise in the room, excitement. Smith didn't hear the cat-soft pad of gun shoes beyond the door. The first he heard was the click of the latch. He dived for the table where he'd left his gun, and was too late.

"Stop!" a voice snapped. "Don't move!"

Smith stopped. His hands well out from his sides, he turned slowly.

HE HAD never seen the man who stood just inside the door, an automatic in his hand, but he recognized him from pictures. Ross McArthur was tall and thin, with thin brownish hair. Rimless glasses blurred watery eyes. Fear had drained his face an unnatural white. His hands shook. His finger was so tight around the trigger that the gun might go off at any instant.

"I heard you say they'd written confessions," he blurted. "I want them. Give them to me quick and let those boys go. I won't shoot unless you cause trouble. But I will if I have to," he said quickly. Terror had made him as dangerous as a hop-head. Sweat stood in thick beads on forehead.

"Sure," Smith said. "I'll get them for you." He moved casually toward the table where the confessions and his gun lay. "How'd you get here?" he asked. He was trying to block McArthur's view of the table.

McArthur said, "I got a tip what was happening." Then he saw the gun. He yelled, "Wait!" His hand was white where it gripped the automatic. The trigger was half back, all the slack gone out of it. Smith knew that any jar, any added fright would send lead ripping through his body.

And then, from the foot of the outside stairway, he heard a soft slurred voice singing:

Now dat my ole dog dead
De rabbits gwiner eat my peas and bread.

McArthur slid across to the table, put Smith's gun in his pocket, then the confessions. He backed away to where Hardick and Tomelli sat tied. With his pocket knife he began to cut them free.

Steps wavered slowly up the stair. The singing voice was very soft.

Ah got a hogeye gal name Lulu Bell—

Hardick and Tomelli shook off their cut ropes, stood up. "We gotta find our guns," Tomelli said. "I ain't leaving this guy alive again." He began to search for the weapons Smith had taken away.

McArthur said, "Hurry up! I want to get out of here." Already he was backing toward the door.

In the hall a voice crooned,

She got hair on her haid lak a horse's mane
An er mouf as big as a table—

Bushelmouth Johnson stood in the doorway. His song cut short. He gazed with consternation at McArthur and the gun.

Hardick yelled, "Look out! The negro!"

McArthur jumped. The gun roared. Smith was spinning and the bullet tugged at his coat. McArthur's gun kept blasting as he whirled toward the door.

Bushelmouth stepped forward. His lips were pulled up in a huge, beatific smile. The sound of his fist striking was as loud as that of the gun.

In the ringing echoes of the shots the noise of the step was buried but Smith heard it. He was still moving and he didn't stop. He dived headlong toward the point where McArthur had fallen. From the rear doorway one shot cracked.

SMITH HIT the floor with one hand on McArthur's gun. He rolled and fired. During years of blindness he'd practiced shooting at sound. But now, rolling, the bullet went wide.

Another shot thundered. He saw McArthur's body jolt, quiver. Smith shot at the light and darkness plunged into the room. From beyond the door he heard the swift clatter of steps. He leaped to his feet, raced after the steps. Over his shoulder he yelled at Bushelmouth to hold Hardick and Tomelli.

The kitchen door was locked. He hammered against it, heard the sound of the back window closing and knew it was too late. He twisted, jumped back for the living room. Pale light filtered into it from the open door. Evidently the two gunmen had tried to make a break past Bushelmouth for they lay placid on the floor now. The girl stood where she had been. Near the door, rigid.

"Get everybody out of here!" Smith snapped at Bushelmouth. "Out the back! The cops will be here in a minute."

"Yassur," Bushelmouth said. He began to load limp bodies over his shoulder. "Dat's two bucks in one night. Hot damn! Business sho is eloquent."

"Come on," Smith said to Marion. "You're going too."

Carl Heikle said into the telephone, "Mr. O'Brien's not here tonight. He's an awfully busy man, you know, awfully busy. Tries to look after everything for his constituents himself, tries to do it personally. You see, it keeps him mighty—"

"I know," Smith said. "It keeps him busy." He could picture O'Brien's big blond secretary resting the telephone on his ample stomach, tilting back in his chair.

Smith said, "I've got two written confessions saying that Ross McArthur hired Hardick and Tomelli to commit those gambling murders. I took them up to my office and persuaded them to sign. But O'Brien or the real head of the parole system, somebody, saw them come there and tipped off McArthur. He wanted McArthur to do the dirty work, but followed and came in the back to make sure. When McArthur failed, this fellow killed him.

"MURDERED!" HEIKLE said. "That's too bad. Too bad."

"Yeah, isn't it. But everybody knows that McArthur took orders from O'Brien. If the papers get these confessions, the resulting stench will knock Pete O'Brien right out of his office."

"Why, er—er...."

"But if O'Brien will stand aside and let Hardick and Tomelli go to the chair—we've got their guns, the ones they used for the killings, and enough evidence without the confessions. O'Brien's got power enough to get those men free, but not enough to keep in office if he does it. Is it a deal?"

"Why, er, of course, I couldn't...."

"Of course," Smith said, "Mr. O'Brien looks after those things personally. If he agrees, let him mention it in the personal column of the *Democrat* tomorrow. I think he'll agree."

Smith read the morning paper with much satisfaction. In the personal column a line said:

> Plan okay; let the boy toast. Pete.

Most of the front page was divided between two stories. Lieutenant Paul Rutgers had caught the murderers he'd been after. He'd captured them single handed in a vacant house on the outskirts of his precinct, handcuffed them and gone out to call the wagon.

When he returned he'd found them chained to chairs with the bodies of their victims on a table between them. The bodies had been stolen from the morgue. Pinned to each man's chest was the sign:

CROOKED POLITICS PAROLED
THIS CRIMINAL
But
THE ELECTRIC CHAIR GIVES NO PAROLE

Another story dealt with the murder of Ross McArthur, prominent politician. His body had been found in the very heart of the city, and the papers were demanding that Rutgers he sent back to headquarters to take this case.

On page twelve was a one-stick story saying the police had been notified of a disturbance in an apartment house on Gentilly Road, but investigation had found no sign of violence. The occupant had been shooting firecrackers, they believed. The police who had answered that call, like the vast majority, had been honest. Rutgers had got in touch with them. They hated the parole system as much as John Smith, and were glad to help.

"Well, I've got those confessions," Smith thought. That would be a little evidence when the final showdown came. And it should come soon. He knew O'Brien was connected with the system, but Smith still needed proof.

He began to wonder about the girl. Sometimes her tips worked, sometimes they almost got him murdered. He couldn't figure her out. But the crooks would know now that she had helped him. She'd had to move into another apartment, but even so they might find her.

"If they do anything to her," he said fiercely, "If—" He was suddenly afraid. He wondered where she was now.

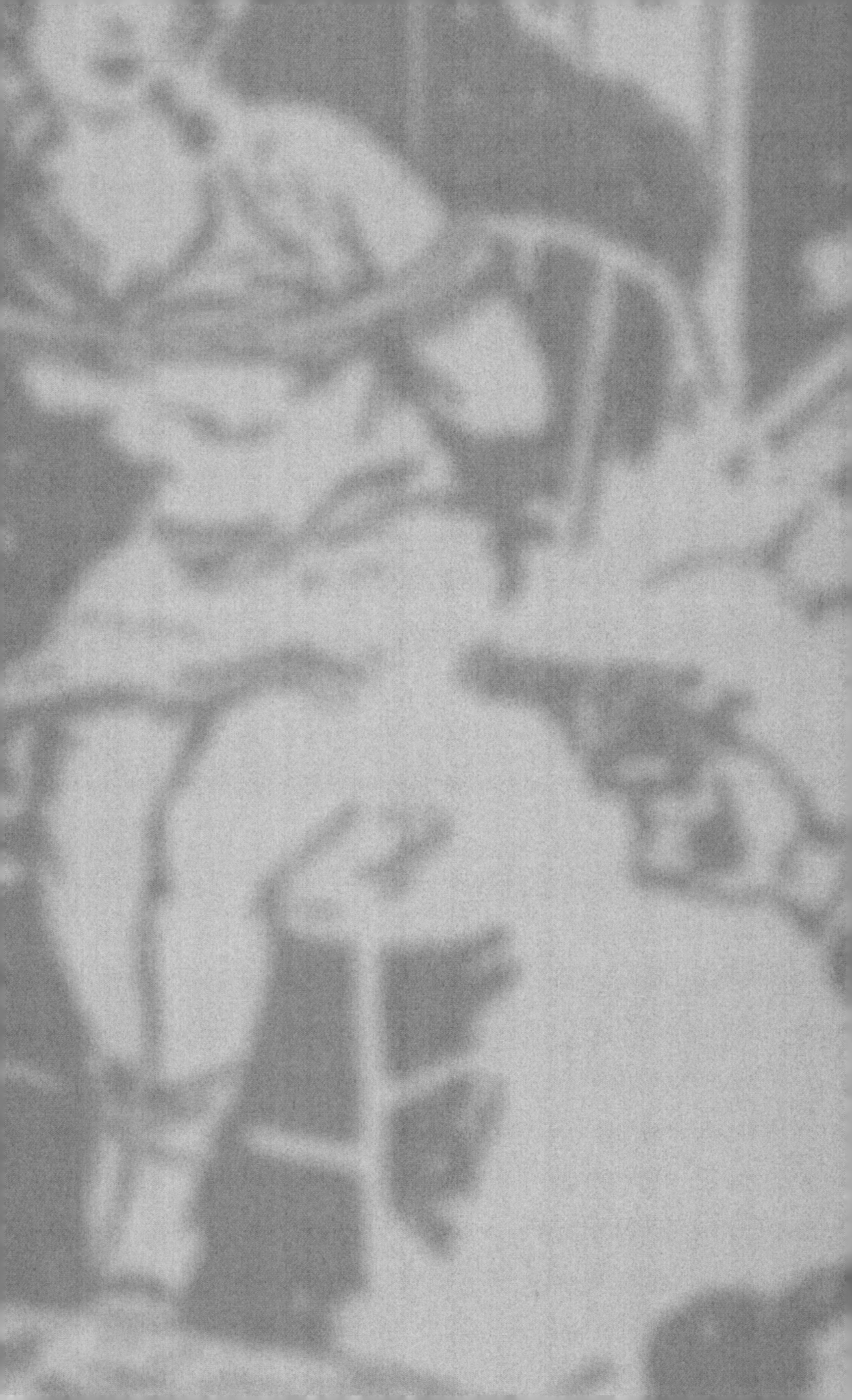

DEATH TRAP FOR THE PAROLE KILLER

Never before had John Smith known such black despair. If he refused the killers' demands, Marion Dark—whose lips had been pressed to his only a few short hours before—would surely die. And if he accepted: he would be walking into a trap from which there could be no escape! But the Parole Killer had never refused a challenge....

CHAPTER ONE
THE SILENT ROOM

THE ROOM trembled to a gigantic but soft tread, and without looking around, Smith said, "I'd like a Scotch and soda, Bushelmouth."

He sat before the open window, barefooted, without shirt or undershirt, thankful that night had come and he could raise the curtain. It had been pulled all day, despite the heat, and through a tucked-back corner he had looked down at the doorway across the street—the same doorway that he had been watching for over a month.

Bushelmouth said, "Yossur. I'll fetch it." He grinned, and the expanse of teeth that showed in the gloom was startling. "But 't won't do no good to drink hit," he said. "Hit only pops back on yo' face in sweat befo' hit can git down you th'oat to do de belly some good." He wiped a huge hand across his forehead, sighed, and went back into the kitchen. He had to duck to get through the low doorway and his shoulders filled it from side to side.

Behind Smith the phone jangled. He turned fast, coming out of his chair and reaching the phone in one easy movement. He was a small man, but compact, and his moves were made with a speed that was deceptive. He was thinking that only two persons knew this number—and neither of them would use it except in an emergency.

Smith said, "Hello."

The big man dived straight at Smith....

The voice on the wire said, "Listen! Listen, Smith! This is Smith?"

"Yes."

"You've got to come out here. Right away. There's something happened and—and...."

"And you're afraid," Smith thought. Aloud he said, "Can you explain?"

"Not over the phone. Somebody called, claimed to be a reporter, and asked if I—if I was sponsoring you in your campaign against the parole racket."

"You told them?"

"I denied it, of course. But I'm afraid something has leaked out. There was another call. A certain man is going to come here tonight. I—I'm afraid he's found out."

"Who is he?"

"Not over the phone. I'd like you to be here. But he may have men watching…." There was terror in the man's voice.

"When is this fellow supposed to get there?" Smith said calmly.

"Right away."

"I'll be over."

"For God's sake be careful! If they see you, you're as good as dead!"

"They won't see me," Smith said. He hung up. He said to Bushelmouth, "Damn it, get me that Scotch."

"Yossur."

SMITH SLID out of his white trousers into dark gray ones that wouldn't show so clearly against the night. He put on a dark shirt, a shoulder holster that held a .38 revolver under his right arm, a dark coat. He dressed without turning on the light, and always he watched the doorway across the street. On the glass over that door was painted

13th ASSEMBLY DISTRICT CLUB

Bushelmouth brought the drink and Smith took it and said, "Keep your eye on that door while I'm gone. Whoever goes in and out, you write it down. You know the ones I'm interested in."

"Yossur. Hit'll be a pure pleasure to get in front dis window."

Smith stepped to the door, leaned close against it, and listened. For thirty seconds he stood without moving, catching only one breath during that time. Then he turned the lock, flipped back the extra bolt, and stepped through into a dimly lighted corridor. There was no one in the hall; he had known there wouldn't be. His ears, which had led him through ten years of blindness before an operation had restored his sight, ears trained to the sensitivity of an animal's, had told him the hall was empty.

A small coupé stood in the alley behind the house, and he lifted the hood, flicked the beam of a flash over the wiring before he got into the car and drove off. Men have been killed before by bombs connected to the starter: and there were hundreds of men in New Orleans who would have put one in Smith's car if they had had the chance.

The house he wanted was a large, white-pillared place on St. Charles. It sat well back from the street, the lawns shadowed by magnolias. Through the trees he could see dim lights behind curtained windows. There was only one car in front and Smith knew it belonged to Claude Vignaux, the man who lived here, the man who had phoned him.

Smith drove past, went down St. Charles for six blocks, circled, and came back toward the house again. He parked in front of the house next door as though he lived there and went whistling up the walk.

There was nobody on the front porch. He ceased to whistle. He went up the front steps quietly, but casually. A watcher would have thought that he was coming home from a day's work.

Once in the darkness of the porch, Smith ducked, slid around to the side and went over the railing. Across the wide lawn that joined this house with Vignaux's he was no more than a scudding shadow, invisible from the street. Then he was standing underneath a window of Vignaux's home.

He crouched there until his ears told him the room was vacant. The window was already open, but screened. He got the screen up—it had been built to move silently—and five seconds later he was inside the house.

HE HAD entered this way before and knew the room, but darkness made little difference to John Smith. On silent, rubber-soled shoes he crossed to where a yellow thread of light marked the door which opened from this room onto the center hall. Once more he paused.

It was then he heard another door open somewhere along the hall outside. He straightened his ears for the sound of voices. There was none.

The person who had opened the other door stood motionless for a moment, then stepped out into the hall. The door closed softly. The person went along the hallway. In the dead stillness Smith heard each step distinctly. It was a curious uneven tread, as though the person who made it were walking with a slight limp.

To the blind a person's walk is as individual as handwriting to one who can see, and Smith knew that the man in the hallway wasn't Claude Vignaux. The visitor Vignaux had expected? Probably. Smith's left hand went under his coat and closed on the butt of the .38. His right hand circled the doorknob, twisted gently.

The door slid open silently. Smith leaned forward until one eye was beyond the sill—and in that moment the man turned a corner in the hallway and was out of sight. Smith heard him cross the living room, heard the front door open and close.

Smith started after him, and stopped. He couldn't afford to be seen here, and Vignaux would tell him who the man was. He had come out of Vignaux's study, the room where Smith and the politician always met.

Smith went along the hallway to the study door and was reaching for the knob when he stopped. His ears, straining against the quiet, excluded the drifting noises of street traffic, the sound of a radio playing next door. He was listening for noises within the house, and there were none. He heard only the whisper of his own breathing, the pounding of his heart. Vignaux should have been here, and yet.... Sudden cold trickled like a feather along Smith's spine.

He opened the study door, took one fast step over the sill. And them he stopped. His eyes, that were round and blue and had been taught by blindness to see, took in the room with the accuracy of a photograph.

Claude Vignaux was sitting behind a rather ornate rosewood desk, his face resting on the desktop, arms dangling limp. A table lamp reflected on his bald head in glistening lights.

Smith did not speak, did not step toward him. The awful intense silence hammered at his ears and told him the truth.

Claude Vignaux was dead.

CHAPTER TWO
DEATH FOR REWARD

"**MURDERED,**" **SMITH** said aloud. His face was ugly and twisted with passion. "Murdered! While I squatted back in that room and let the killer walk away!" His lean, flexible hands knotted in front of him. A lump rose in his throat.

He stared at Vignaux, seeing the man as he had never seen him in life. He had been pompous, affected, but that was simply the manner of the old-time politician. He had possessed courage of the greatest and noblest kind. Some men do heroic deeds without a tremor, without ever knowing the meaning of the word "fear." But inability to feel fear is not necessarily bravery. Vignaux had been afraid, terribly afraid, since the day, two years ago, he had hired Smith to break the vicious parole racket. And yet he had kept on with the fight. He had known fear, and gone ahead despite it. That was true courage.

Smith's voice was very soft, no louder than the faint breeze against the curtains. "I'll get the man who killed you," he said. "I'll carry on the fight!"

It came to him suddenly that death was the inevitable end for any man who fought the parole system. It was too-well-entrenched to be broken. Vignaux was dead. Sooner or later the men who sought for Smith, the hundreds of criminals and the crooked politicians who fattened on criminality, would find him. There would be a short blaze of guns—and Smith too would die.

"But until that time," Smith said, "until then…" His face, with the sleepless lines under his eyes and the twisted mouth, was terrible.

He moved until his back was against the wall and he could see the whole room at once, and he stood there studying it. There was no sign that anyone had been here except Vignaux. Everything was normal except for the limp body upon the desk. The feet had slipped backward slightly, the right trouser cuff pulling up so that he could see the rolled sock and dangling garter, the flabby flesh of the ankle. The lax hands hung close to the feet.

He went over the room carefully, but there was nothing else. Nothing to work on. "And I let the killer walk away," he thought.

No normal man would have heard the front door open. There was only the faintest squeak. Then furtive, cautious footsteps in the living room. They came into the corridor, hesitated. They moved stealthily toward the study door.

Smith's lips were thin across his teeth now. His left hand dipped under his coat and came out with the .38. Two long strides carried him across the room to where the opening door would shield him. Bent from the waist, the gun steady in his hand, he waited.

He saw the knob turn. He heard the faint click of the latch. The door crept open.

A girl stepped over the sill. She had blonde hair that curled like a halo round her head. Her face was small and heart-shaped and cherubic. She wasn't tall, but she was as tall as Smith and very delightfully fashioned.

Smith said, "Marion!"

She jumped, her mouth open on a short cry that never sounded. Her eyes were startled for a moment. Then she grinned. "You jack-in-the-box," she said. "You pop up everywhere I turn." Then she nodded at Vignaux and asked, "What's wrong with him?"

"He was murdered."

Marion Dark's eyes got wide, then narrow with thoughts moving swiftly behind them. There was no hint of fear in her face. A coroner couldn't have accepted death more casually. "Well, I'll be damned," she said. "Who did it?"

"**THE PAROLE** system," Smith said. There was no longer any reason to hide the fact that it was Vignaux who had hired the "Parole Killer"—as Smith was known from end to end of the underworld—and had started that mysterious figure m his war upon a savage racket. Now, even in death, Vignaux would fight the racket. His death would once more blazon the abuse of parole across the front pages of the nation. Public indignation, growing daily, would mount toward that climactic point where it would sweep the old corruption out of office and demand honesty from its officials.

"The parole system murdered him," Smith said again. "Put that in your paper. Tell them you had an interview with the Parole Killer and that's what he told you."

Surprise showed in her face. "How did you know I…?"

"Worked for a newspaper? I'm supposed to be a detective. And you keep hanging around. I had to find out about you."

"And now… You mean… Hot damn! Hand me that phone!"

Smith got it first. "Wait a minute," he said. "I want to know what you're doing here."

When she smiled she looked like an angel. He could never reconcile the girl's personality with her face. "I knew there was somebody backing you," she said. "I had an idea it was Vignaux—he was on the parole board and his son was killed by a paroled convict just before you opened your campaign. I'd been checking on him. I telephoned him tonight, but he just denied it. So I came out. I didn't think he'd like to give me an interview, so I walked in without ringing."

"Okay," Smith said.

"Gimme that phone!"

"One more thing," he said. He called police headquarters and asked for Lieutenant Paul Rutgers. Rutgers and Vignaux were the only men who had known from the first that Smith was the Parole Killer; they were the only persons who knew his hideout and the phone number that could reach him.

Now he explained to Rutgers what had happened. "Mrs. Vignaux and the servants are gone," he said. "Probably Vignaux sent them out earlier."

"It'll take me about nine minutes," Rutgers said. He paused. "Maybe you better be gone when I get there. There are always some crooked cops. They'd murder you as quickly as any of O'Brien's gunmen."

"I'll be gone," Smith said.

"Give me that damn phone," Marion said. "After this story I ought to make more than the city editor!"

Smith caught her as she started forward, turned her around to face him. "Listen. There's one thing about that story. You've got to write it, tell your editor, everybody, that I telephoned you, that you've never seen me."

"Why?"

"You fool," he said. "There are men who have seen you helping me. If O'Brien or his killers knew where to find you—" He stopped. He was afraid to finish the sentence. Terror squeezed at his heart.

"Would it matter to you?" she asked softly, looking up at him.

He swallowed and turned sharply away from her. "There've been enough persons killed already without dragging in a newspaper reporter," he said.

He didn't look at her again. He was conscious of her watching him for a long while before she turned and went out.

Smith searched the room again, making sure he had missed nothing. Police sirens were wailing on St. Charles when he slid out of the window he had entered.

BUSHELMOUTH JOHNSON let him into the small, furnace-hot apartment across from the 13th District Club. "Ah seen dat Mistur Pete O'Brien, de monkey-face man," Bushelmouth said. "Jes 'bout twenty minutes past he gits out dat car down yonder and goes in de do' cross de street. He's de one who's head rooster in dis parole business, ain't he?"

"I don't know," Smith said. "If he's not the top, he's close to it. Get me a drink."

He slipped out of his coat, loosened his tie and collar. He felt tired all the way through. The strain of these last few months had changed him more than the slight disguise of dyeing his blond hair brown and growing a moustache. There were deep circles under his eyes and his face was pulled into hard, bitter angles. He was a bow drawn too tight and held that way. Only by conscious physical effort could he relax the fierce tension of his nerves.

Bushelmouth came back to find Smith at the window again, taking up his constant, hopeless vigil. "Lawd, Mistur Smiff! You sho look in de dozens. Somebody dead?"

"The man who hired me," Smith said.

"Well, ah swear. De way folks been kilt roun' here since you took dis parole job hit's ar wonder dere ain't a waitin' line at de cemetary. Fo' er five times I done figgered I wuz dead. But I ain't."

"Not from the head down," Smith said. He tried to grin. He sipped deep at his drink and lay back in hrs chair, letting the tired feeling run soft and relaxed through his body. But always his eyes were on the doorway across the street. There would never be any real rest until he had caught the man who killed Claude Vignaux, until he had broken the whole filthy system.

It was a half-hour later that the phone rang. Lieutenant Rutgers' voice said, "Hey, I thought you told me Vignaux was murdered."

"He was."

"Then how? There's not a mark on him, except that bruise on his forehead, and Doc McGreer thinks that was made after he died. He thinks it was heart failure, and Vignaux slumped forward and struck his head on the desk. There's no evidence of poison."

"He was killed," Smith said stubbornly.

"How did you know?"

Smith wet his lips. "I don't know," he said. "It's just one of those hunches. But there was nothing wrong with Vignaux's heart."

His mind turned back, recalling the picture of that room as vividly as though he looked at a photograph. No evidence anywhere of an intruder, although he had seen a man leaving. He thought of the lights gleaming on the bald head, the hands hanging limply by the feet.

"By God!" he snapped "That's it! That's how he was killed!"

"How?"

"That dangling sock on the right ankle! Not a man who dressed as fastidiously as Claude Vignaux!"

"What do you mean?" Rutgers said, but his voice was fast now.

"Tell Doc McGreer to look for novocaine, among other things. It kills fast, is almost impossible to find by a routine autopsy. And it's easy to get."

"I'll tell him." Rutgers was about to hang up when he checked himself, said, "By the way. That blonde girl-friend of yours has been hounding me. She says she's got to get in touch with you."

"Thanks. But I don't think I want to see her." He hung up.

HE HAD lied, and he knew it. Since the first time Marion Dark had walked into his office, he'd found himself wanting to see her, more and more often. But a man in his work couldn't have friends. It would only put himself and them in added danger. Still....

He didn't mean to go and see her. He was surprised when he found himself in her apartment.

She had never been so pretty. In the shadowed lights her hair was pale and shimmering. Her face seemed pale too as she stood in the middle of the floor for a long minute and looked at him. Then she came close. Her hands were on the lapels of his coat. She said, "John. I had to see you."

"Yes?" He was conscious of the sound of his own heart, of the feel of it hammering against his ribs.

"You don't have to go on with this fight any more, do you, John? You are through with it now?"

"Through?" he said. "I'm just getting started. The people are getting aroused now. And with Vignaux's murder—"

"That's what I mean," she said quickly. "They killed him. They found out he was backing you. And they—they'll kill you."

"They haven't yet," he said.

Her hands clenched on his coat and she shook him. "You idiot!" she cried. "You know you can't go on forever! The odds are too great. Sooner or later they'll find you, John. And when they do...."

"But I can't stop," he said. "It's my job."

"It's not! Vignaux hired you. He's dead now. Nobody is asking you to carry on the fight."

"Somebody's got to," Smith said. His voice was husky and fierce with emotion. "You know how rotten the system is. You know that practically every major criminal the country has produced recently has been let out of jail on parole. Dillinger, Floyd, Nelson, Karpis—all of them!

"I know, but...."

"I've got a score of my own," Smith said. A forefinger traced the dim scar across his forehead. "A bullet from a paroled convict's gun put that scar on me. I was blind for ten years. Try sitting in the dark for ten years, thinking you'll never see again."

"But you've settled that," she said desperately. "And the abuse of parole is not your duty alone. It's society's duty. If society wants to sit back and sleep and let crooked politicians make prison gates into turnstiles where bandits and murderers and rapists can pass through and out again, that's society's business. Why should you carry the fight alone?"

"But I—I started, and...."

She interrupted. "You don't even have a job any longer. Vignaux's not alive to hire you. All you will get will be—death."

Her face was white now, her lips trembling. "Don't you see? If you keep on with this and they kill you—I...."

"You mean you...."

"You idiot," she said. "You damned idiot!"

Then somehow he had his arms around her and her arms were tight around him and their lips clung together. They swayed, holding hard to one another.

She pulled away, only far enough to look at him. "You may be a fair detective," she said; "but you're damn slow in learning about women. For the last month I've been wondering when you'd kiss me. And now I practically have to lasso you."

"Perhaps I'm still blind," he said. "I always think I am when I look at you. I remember how I'd sit in the dark and try to picture women, thinking all the time that I'd never see one again. And so I would try to imagine them prettier than a living woman could ever be. And I remember when you first walked into my office and I thought I was blind again because I was seeing what I had dreamed of so often."

She kissed him again. She said, "You are hard to start, but you accelerate fast."

WOMAN-LIKE SHE knew when she had the advantage and she used it. She said, "You don't want to die now."

"Die?" He had forgotten their argument. He held her close against him. "I'm just starting to live!"

"Then you will quit this hopeless fight? You will leave town?"

She saw the change in his face. "It's because I love you," she said swiftly. "And you can't keep on like this. Even if they don't find you and kill you, you can't stand the strain much longer. You look like a ghost of yourself. Even without your hair dyed brown, I'd hardly know you. Say you'll quit. Say you'll change your name and go to some other town. I'll come with you. We'll go somewhere, anywhere."

He hesitated, his mouth open to say the words. He held the girl fiercely against him, feeling the need of her run like liquid fire through his blood.

"Promise," she said.

"I—"

The phone rang sharply.

The girl answered and a moment later as she turned to Smith her face was white. "It's Paul Rutgers. Don't speak to him, John. Don't!"

"Why?"

"It'll be something awful. I know! I feel it! Don't speak to him!"

"But I'll have to talk to him," he said. He lifted the phone from the table.

"I called your place," Rutgers' voice said. "When Bushelmouth told me you were gone I had an idea where to get you."

"Smart, huh?"

"I've got a message for you. Claude Vignaux's lawyer had a letter to give me in case anything happened to Vignaux. My letter was really a note to you."

"Yes?"

"There's ten thousand in cash—for work yet to be done. You understand?"

"I understand."

He never remembered replacing the receiver or turning until he saw the girl. He only remembered her face, the blood draining from it, the eyes too wide and horrible, the teeth biting into her lip.

"I can't quit the parole fight," he said. "Claude Vignaux is still hiring me. He gave his life to crush the racket. I can't break faith with him now."

She didn't speak. She only looked at him and he stared dumbly back at her. It was more than his life now that he was staking against impossible odds. There was her love and her happiness.

He said, "I have a phone where you can reach me. Don't use it unless you have to. It's not safe. I won't be back here until—until I'm free." He gave her the number. He looked at her for a long moment, impressing her picture upon his mind so that he might carry it with him. Then he turned and went out of the room.

CHAPTER THREE
KIDNAPED!

THE DRAGGING eternity of the next day drove Smith half insane. He had a wild desire to go out and in one terrible blast clean up the whole mess.

But how? Which way could he turn? So far it was not even proved that Vignaux had been murdered.

All he had to work on was the knowledge that Pete O'Brien, nominally only the leader of the 13th District but actually one of the most powerful political figures in the state, was connected with the parole racket. Whether or not he was the mysterious figure that controlled it, that sold paroles to criminals in return for the profits of crime, that forced politicians to obey his orders by threats of blackmail and death, Smith couldn't be sure.

He had to fight the impulse to storm across the street and into O'Brien's office, and beat the truth from him and murder the criminals and gangsters and crooked politicians who fattened upon the racket. That was the way they would have worked. They planned to kill Smith on sight. But he had to stay within the law.

It was nearly dark when Rutgers phoned. "You were right," he said. "Novocaine. But knowing that won't help us much. It's too easy to get. I've got half my men working on it, but there's little hope."

"We'll make hope!" Smith said. His fingers tightened convulsively around the phone. His face set. "Call the papers," he said. "Tell them the murder happened this way: the killer knew Vignaux and Vignaux was expecting him. The man slugged him on the forehead, just hard enough to knock him out. Then he took down a sock and injected novocaine into one of the veins at the ankle. He waited until Vignaux was plenty dead—he'd die in about thirty seconds after the injection—and shoved his head down on the desk. This was so the bruise would look as if it were made after death by Vignaux falling. The killer didn't want it to be known as murder because he didn't want any more front page stories about parole."

"That's probably the way it was," Rutgers admitted. "But why print it?"

"Tell the papers that you know all this because Parole Killer described it to you. Hint that he *saw* the murder, but for some reason was unable to prevent it. Hint that he told you who the killer is, and that you are trying to get some physical proof that will stand up in court."

"The idea," Rutgers said slowly, "being to push the murderer into an error, to send him looking for you more than before." Smith heard the policeman swallow hard. "It will be condemning you to death," Rutgers said.

"They have already condemned me," Smith said. "But they haven't executed the sentence."

It was five minutes after ten when his phone rang again. He picked it up, thinking Rutgers must have found a lead of some kind. But it wasn't Rutgers' voice he heard. It was a woman's voice—a voice so deformed by emotion that at first he couldn't recognize it. "John," it said. "John, I— I… The words broke on a sob.

He said, "Hello? Who…?" And then terror struck him like a blow over the heart. He tried to speak and his mouth worked without sound. "Marion," he said finally. "Marion, what's wrong?"

There was a moment of empty silence. The voice on the wire said, "Nothing. Nothing. I just… And then the words came with a fierce, desperate rush, "They know and are—" He heard a muffled *plop* that might have been an open hand striking hard against flesh. He caught the husk of a man's voice saying, "Damn you, you little…" There was a sharp click as the connection was broken.

SMITH STOOD holding his phone, listening at the drone of an empty line.

He put down the instrument and it seemed to him that he moved very slowly like a man struggling through deep water. His brain was screaming, "Hurry! Hurry!" and the slowness of actuality tortured him; yet with that same unbroken movement he had turned, caught up shoulder holster and gun and coat and leaped for the door.

Bushelmouth popped his head out of the kitchen doorway. "Law' god, Mistur Smiff, what's done happen? You…" He was speaking to a swinging door and an empty corridor. From the alley came the sound of a motor leaping into action.

Smith raced the little car across town. He was not thinking, not planning ahead, even to the next automobile that he must dodge. Something had happened to Marion—his brain had congealed on that one thought. He had to get there, get there quick.

She had an apartment in the old French Quarter near St. Peter's. He brought the coupé roaring down St. Claude and when a motorcycle cop swung out behind him, he cut left, then right, then left again and right once more, so swiftly the cop was lost. His tires screamed on corners. A sedan swung out from the curb in front of him and he went up on the opposite walk making sixty-three. There was a rending crash. He skidded, went sideways, and was straight again by a miracle, his right back fender swinging loose and machine-gunning against tire and body.

It was mad, insane driving. He felt no terror, no emotion at all. He was hypnotized by the one frozen thought in his brain. He had to reach Marion.

He was a block from her apartment when the loose fender was caught between the back tire and another automobile and the tire blew out. The car swerved. Smith had the door open, hit the running-board, the street, and was sprinting away before the car had completely stopped.

It was one of those buildings, common in the French Quarter, where the front entrance looks like a crack in a solid brick wall. There was a passageway, semi-dark and so narrow he could touch both walls at once, and then he came into a wide, flagged courtyard with a fountain in the center. Buildings rose to left and right joined by a high brick wall that formed the opposite side of the court.

He was still running, head lifted so that he could see the little balcony and French window that marked Marion's second-floor apartment. The balcony was dark, the window behind it dark. He didn't cut toward the building's entrance, but went straight across the court, running without sound on rubber-soled shoes. He jumped, his fingers closed on the top of the brick wall and he swung himself up. He was running along the top of the wall before he was fully erect.

The balcony was about two feet higher than the wall, and ten feet from it. He judged his distance in those last six short strides while he gained speed. And then he jumped.

He seemed to hang in the air a while. His feet were outthrust, and looking over them he thought he was going to miss. If he dropped an inch or two more....

His toes hit the edge of the balcony. His knees bent, bringing his body closer but it was still far back of his feet. His arms were stretched, his hands reached for the rail and were inches short. His left foot slipped from the balcony. He began to fall.

It was that which brought him close enough for his fingers to catch the rail. He hung an instant that was ages long, then began to pull himself up.

There was a sound like that of a cat screaming and the balcony rail bent outward as nails pulled loose. Still clutching a segment of it, he plunged downward.

HIS HEELS hit the court first, then his whole body seemed to strike at once, from feet to head. The jar threatened to bounce his heart and lungs from their place, but there was no pain. His brain seemed to turn slowly over under his skull and his eyes staring upward saw the balcony's edge revolve round and round through the semi-dark.

And then a man was on the balcony with a gun in his hand. He aimed down at Smith for a long while. And fired.

Smith didn't know he was moving. It seemed to him that the whole world was turning. The red and yellow flame lancing down at him hurt his eyes. He closed them, still twisting along the ground. His left hand had dipped under his coat and come out with the revolver.

Shooting straight downward makes for poor marksmanship. The man on the balcony had missed his first shot. The second one left a bloody trench along Smith's right cheek. Then Smith had his own gun out. His eyes were closed. He fired upward at the sound of the shot.

For ten years of his blindness, Smith had practiced shooting at sound. Now the gun recoiled once in his hand. The echoes drifted out across the court. They beat back and forth for a moment, and were still. In the silence he heard the crack of an automatic striking the pavement. Smith opened his eyes to see a man poised in the air above him as though hung by some invisible cord. A long while he hung there. Then the cord snapped. The man crashed face down upon the flagstones.

The pieces of Smith's brain jolted together again, though his heart still hurt and there was little air in his lungs. In the neighboring buildings, blinds banged open. Voices sounded.

On hands and knees Smith reached the body. He had his gun in his right hand now, his fountain pen in his left and he scrawled on the pavement at the man's head, the single word PAROLE. There was no time for more. He was inside the building and running up steps toward Marion's apartment. His knees wobbled under him.

Two men looked out of their doors and saw him. They saw the blue eyes glittering and wild, the set of his mouth. They saw the blood running thick along his cheek. And neither of those men spoke or tried to interfere.

He reached Marion's door, slammed it with his shoulder as his right hand twisted the knob. It banged open and he was over the sill into darkness. He spun so that his body would not show against the lighted door, and waited.

For once his ears failed him. Blood pounded against his eardrums and he could hear nothing else. His own breathing was a series of racking sobs. His heart hurt.

Always the dark had given him the advantage, but now it was the other way around. He knew where the light switch was and he jumped for it. The white glare blinded him and he turned, blinking, crouched above his gun.

The room was empty.

He went through the apartment fast. But there was no one else there. Marion was gone!

THE BUILDING and court were in an uproar now. He could hear someone shouting, "Here, Officer! This way. Right up there!" He got one fast glimpse from the balcony and saw that the leap back to the brick wall was a total impossibility. He whirled again into the living room—and saw the door crowded with white faces!

His mind worked now with cold, swift precision. The cops would have to carry him down to headquarters. Once there, politics would work to hold him. He might go free, might not. And in the meanwhile, what would happen to Marion?

He swung his gun up, leveling it toward the crowded doorway. "All right, I'm shooting!" he yelled. He jumped forward—and when he got to the door it was empty. But a blue cap was bobbing up the stairs and a police whistle shrilled in the court.

He slammed the door, locked it. He'd been here before and knew there was a dumbwaiter. It was on the ground floor, but it didn't take long to get it up. Outside, the cop began to hammer on the door and yelled, "Open up! Open up in there!"

"Just a minute," Smith shouted. "I'll open it." Then he was inside the dumbwaiter shaft and pulling himself upward.

It was only a four-story-building. He was at the third floor before the cop began to shout again and pound on the door. He was on the top floor when he heard noises echo up the shaft and knew they'd got the door open. And five seconds later he was on the roof.

The building next door was a story lower than this one, but set flush against it. He hung by his fingers and dropped. While he searched for the stair he tried to mop the blood from his face.

There were three patrol cars at the curb outside. Men and women were running from every direction, but their attention was on the building next door. Smith slid into the first patrol car and drove away at twenty miles an hour.

He had an idea why it had taken the cops so long to open the door, and why, when they had found the apartment vacant, they had not suspected his trick for escaping and tried to head him off. He thought of the single word, PAROLE, scrawled at the dead man's head. The vast majority of the cops were honest: they hated the abuse of parole as intensely as Smith did. They knew the signature of the Parole Killer, and knew that he killed only in self-defense. If they had been a little slow and he managed to escape, they wouldn't worry.

Smith drove carefully, never exceeding the speed limit as he turned out St. Claude again. His mind was like that of a man dead-drunk but who remains to all appearances completely sober—who, concentrating every nerve and fibre on some definite end, is totally blind to consequences and means. He was very calm. He didn't hurry. Yet there was only one thought in his mind. He was going to get Marion free from the men who had kidnaped her. How he did it or what the results, he didn't care.

CHAPTER FOUR
WHEN THE LAW HAS FAILED....

HE PARKED the police coupé in front of the 13th District Club and got out. The trench along his right cheek had ceased to bleed though it stood wide and gaping and the blood had stained the whole side of his face and flowed down over his chin and shirt. He went quietly up the stairs, turned right until he found the door marked PETE O'BRIEN, opened it, and went in.

Carl Heikle, O'Brien's stomachy secretary, was not at his desk in the outer office. But there were two of the boys sitting in overstuffed chairs near the right wall. They looked like a pair of wrestlers; they were actually poll watchers during elections, gunmen, bouncers, and handymen at other times. They stared at Smith, at the blood on his face. One of them lumbered erect, said, "What is it, pal?"

"O'Brien in his office?"

"Yeah, but he's busy. Whatdaya want?"

"I want O'Brien," Smith said. "Who's with him?"

"Ain't nobody with him, he's busy." The man's heavy face wrinkled with thought. "Who are you, pal? Ain't you…?"

"I've had my hair dyed and grown this little mustache," Smith said, "since you got your orders to kill me."

"You—you—"

"I'm John Smith."

The tableau held an instant, then moved on slowly, all together, like a piece of statuary that begins to crack and sway apart. Both of the guards reached for their guns.

Smith did not seem to move as fast as they did, yet the police-special was in his hand before the big men touched their guns. "Don't do it," Smith said. "I didn't come here to kill you, but I will if necessary."

They looked at him and knew he spoke the truth. "All right," Smith said. "Just stay where you are for a moment." He slid past them, silent, until he reached O'Brien's door. He put his right ear against the panel, still watching the gunmen, his own gun in his left hand. They stood there paralyzed with fear, yet Smith was taking no chances. Five seconds he stood there, until his ears told him there was only one man in the room beyond. Then he stepped aside and gestured with the revolver.

"You first," he said softly. The guards went in ahead of him. He followed and closed the door.

O'Brien was working at some papers on his desk. He was, as Bushelmouth had said, a monkey-faced man. He was small and wizened and dark. A thin scattering of black hairs were plastered down against the top of his skull, but most of his head was bald. He wore a white suit, a blue silk shirt, blue tie, and handkerchief in his breast pocket to match. The corner of the handkerchief was worked with an elaborate monogram. He did not look up as Smith followed the two guards into the room. He said, "What is it, Ed?"

Smith said, "It's me."

O'Brien flung back in his chair, head up. Even then his face showed nothing, his emotion buried under the mass of wrinkles that cobwebbed his features. But the small dark eyes were alive and startled and afraid. "You? You…?" And on an outlet of breath, "John Smith!"

"Right," Smith said.

There was a crafty light in the dark eyes now, and less fear. "I'm glad to see you, Mr. Smith. What are you after?"

"You," Smith said.

"Me? What…?"

"I'm taking you along with me." Smith's voice was flat and toneless. He might have been repeating a message that didn't interest him. "I'm going to hold you until tomorrow afternoon, and if by that time Marion Dark hasn't been released, I'm going to murder you."

BLOOD SUDDENLY drained from the wrinkled face leaving it an awful gray as though suddenly it had begun to rot. The thick lips opened and shut, but no sound came forth.

"I'll murder you, and after that, every man that I'm certain is connected with your racket. I'll kill them all—or I'll get that girl back. These may help." Quietly he scooped the papers from O'Brien's desk and stuffed them in his pocket

"You—you can't," O'Brien said. "You are a detective, Mr. Smith. You have sworn to uphold the law. You…."

Once more Smith made that dreadful laughing sound that wasn't laughter at all. "Law?" he said. *"You* talk about the law? Listen. While you stuck to your fight against me, I kept inside the law. You tried to frame me; you tried to frame Paul Rutgers because he helped me—there's no need of covering that now. And I stayed inside the law and fought. But now you've taken a girl, O'Brien. And I'm taking you. Come on."

O'Brien was holding to his desk to keep erect. "You—you can't. You…."

"Shut up. These apes of yours know where the girl is, or can get word to somebody who does. Her release will be printed in the afternoon papers tomorrow. If it's not—" the blue eyes looked calmly at O'Brien— "I'll kill you and look for the next man. Come on."

"I don't know what you are talking about! I haven't—"

"Don't tell me," Smith said. "Just come on." He stepped sideways to leave O'Brien a clear passage to the door and cover the guards at the same time. "You boys stay here. And remember, tomorrow' afternoon—unless you start something before then."

The politician swayed away from his desk. It looked for a moment as though he were going to fall, but he braced himself and his steps were almost steady as he crossed the room. No one spoke. There was no sound except the uneven thud of his shoes on the floor.

Smith heard them and his mind whirled back to a dark room where he had crouched listening to footsteps going swiftly along a dark corridor with a curious, limping walk, footsteps going away from Vignaux's murdered body.

"So you killed him!"

O'Brien was at the door and he turned. "Killed who? What are you talking about?"

"Claude Vignaux," Smith said. "You murdered him."

"I—I—"

"Don't argue. Get out."

The mass of wrinkles that was O'Brien's face twitched. Saliva drooled from the corner of his mouth. He tried to talk without knowing what words he wanted, but Smith waved at the door. Somehow O'Brien opened it and went into the outer office.

They were halfway across the room when it happened. Smith was watching O'Brien, his ears tuned to the office door behind him to make sure the gunmen didn't try to follow. There was another door on the opposite side of the office, standing ajar. The hinges on this door were oiled. They made only the faintest breath of sound as they opened wider.

There was no time for Smith to turn. His gaze leaped upward and in a mirror on the opposite wall he could see a reflection of the door, the thin slit between the wall and the door on the side of the hinges, the black muzzle of an automatic poking through. There was no chance to dodge—only one split second in which to act.

Smith jumped forward and jabbed his gun into the small of O'Brien's back.

O'Brien cried out and staggered. In the mirror Smith saw the gun muzzle swerve uncertainly to follow him, knew that the added weight of a hair upon the trigger was the difference between him and death.

"Hold it!" Smith said. He was surprised that his voice sounded calm and natural when his throat felt swollen. He wondered he could speak at all his mouth was so dry. "Hold it," he said again. "I've got the hammer back on this gun and I'm holding it with my thumb. Shoot me, and O'Brien gets this one in the spine."

O'BRIEN TRIED to turn but Smith had his right hand on his shoulder. So they stood for a moment, until the politician's gaze found the mirror. "Carl?" he croaked. "Is that you, Carl?"

"Yes, sir," Heikle said. "I've been in this office all the time and I thought perhaps you were having some difficulty with Mr. Smith. I started to phone the police, but was reluctant without your permission, as you...."

"For God's sake," O'Brien said. "Don't stand there and jabber all night. Do something!"

"Shoot me?" Smith asked. He shoved his gun hard against O'Brien's back.

"No! No! He'll kill me, Carl!"

"Right," Smith said. He could imagine Heikle back of the door, stomachy, blond, pink-cheeked. Right now it was a draw between them. But things couldn't stay this way long. Any moment the two gunmen might come out of O'Brien's office, or someone might come in from the street. There wouldn't be much chance for Smith then....

Smith's right hand tightened on O'Brien's shoulder. He pulled the politician close against him, then wheeled fast and had the monkey-faced man between him and Heikle before the secretary had time to act. Smith backed toward the outer door, pulling O'Brien with him. He felt his own back touch the doorknob.

And then the door of O'Brien's private office opened and the gunmen came out. They came out fast, their guns drawn.

It happened with the suddenness of an exploding shell. Smith snapped one shot past O'Brien but the politician was pawing at his arm and the bullet went wide. He grabbed the door open with his right hand and in that second of freedom O'Brien was leaping away from him, shouting. Then Smith was outside the door, feeling it shudder to the impact of bullets. He whirled and plunged down the stair.

The street was well lighted with persons passing in both directions, but seemingly no one had heard the shots. Glancing up, Smith saw the dark blot of his own window directly opposite. He strolled toward it. Down the street he heard the newsboys shouting the bulldog editions of the morning papers with the story Rutgers had given them. "Vignaux proved murdered! Parole Killer witnesses killing! *The Mawnin' Times!*"

He was stepping on the far sidewalk looking back over his shoulder, when he saw the gunmen come out of the door he'd just left. He gave no sign of seeing them, but merged with a group of persons strolling toward the corner. It wasn't likely they'd shoot in public just after they'd been seen to leave the club, but he took no chances.

The gunmen kept on their side of the street and some ten yards behind. At the corner Smith turned quickly. This street was darker than St. Claude and by the time he'd gone twenty feet the night wrapped itself around him, dark, silent.

The gunmen followed him across St. Claude. A thin, set smile came on Smith's mouth. His left hand went under his coat and came out with the long-barreled revolver and he balanced it, testing its weight. His jaw muscles bulged hard, crooking his mouth.

There were two against one. Either of them was almost twice as large as Smith and they meant to kill him, while he wanted them alive. But he was in no position to pick his odds.

He walked quietly, keeping to the thick shadows. The killers were thirty yards behind, but on the quiet street he could catch the sound of their steps. He didn't need to look back now; he could place them by the click-click of their heels.

The narrow alley which ran back of his apartment loomed up, but all Smith's energies were centered on those steps behind him. He had no warning of what was going to happen until the hand closed on his shoulder and lifted him. It swung him like a child clear of the ground and into the alley.

HE WAS twisting while his feet were in the air. The gun in his left hand swung up. His finger tightened on the trigger. Then he was looking into the enormous expanse of Bushelmouth Johnson's white teeth.

Smith's muscles went watery and he sagged. "Damn you!" he whispered. "I almost blew you full of holes."

Bushelmouth made an elaborate gesture of silence. He stooped until his mouth was close to Smith's ear. "Dere's er pair of dem O'Brien guntoters followin' you, Mistur Smiff. Ah seen 'em frum de window and ah thought ah'd sneak down an' wahn you." He stared at Smith's face. "What's done happen? A wreck?"

Under his breath Smith said, "Call it that."

He could hear the steps now, not ten yards away. The man O'Brien had called Ed, whispered, "Where'd the guy go, Nick?"

"I don't know. And I hope I don't find out."

Smith pulled Bushelmouth's head close. "I want 'em," he said. "Alive. I'll take the one on this side; you get the other."

"Yossur." A white spot showed in the dark. It stretched wider and unbelievably wider as Bushelmouth's grin bared his teeth.

The steps were close now. Three yards, two, one yard away. Smith held the butt of his gun shoulder high, the barrel upward. Bushelmouth had licked the fingers of his left hand and was rubbing them across the knuckles of his right fist. The two gunmen showed at the alley mouth.

Smith took one sharp step and went up on his toes. Even then the man was nearly a foot above him. He swung the gun.

It was Ed on Smith's side, and Ed never had any warning before the gun barrel slapped his head and he went down. Bushelmouth was stepping around him and Nick heard the movement and swung. He turned far enough for his jaw to offer a perfect landing for Bushelmouth's fist. It struck with all Bushelmouth's two hundred and thirty pounds behind it, and the killer spun, slammed down on his face, skidded across the walk into the street. After that he didn't move.

Bushelmouth licked his knuckles and rubbed them. "Mah hands gittin' soft," he lamented. "Ah could feel dat when ah hit him."

"I doubt if Nick could," Smith said. "Gather 'em up and bring them in. I want to talk to them."

"Yossur."

Ed was beginning to stir, so Bushelmouth rapped him one on the jaw. He flung one man over one shoulder and one over the other and followed Smith down the alley. In the apartment Smith pulled down the curtains, turned on the light, and told Bushelmouth to tie the prisoners. He was doing so when he found their guns.

He said, "Mistur Smiff, dis gentlemun ah hit got er fo'ty-fo'."

"Sure," Smith said.

"He ain't had hit in his hand, but he almos' did."

"Sure," Smith said. He had his back turned, dressing the wound in his cheek.

Bushelmouth sighed. "Ah reckon tha' don't count," he said. And added hopefully, "Not even fo' bits worth?"

"What do you mean? Worth of what?"

"I sweah, Mister Smiff, don you know what you said, Mistur Smiff. 'Bout if I see a man pint a gun at you and ah hit him 'fo he shoots, you'd gimme a buck fer some Bay St. Louis cawn. You know ah don't like dis legal moufwash lak you drinks."

"Okay," Smith said, and laughed. "He didn't point the gun, but that wasn't his fault. I'll make it a buck anyway." He handed it over.

"Hotdamn! Ain't had me no cawn since de Lawd hisself can't remember when."

"What's that odor on your breath?"

"Aw, Mistur Smiff...."

"Okay," Smith said. "But get some water for these gentlemen. I want to talk to them."

CHAPTER FIVE
BAIT FOR THE KILLER'S TRAP

SMITH HAD only one question to ask: Where was Marion Dark? He asked it repeatedly, and with emphasis. Finally he was convinced they didn't know.

"All right," he said. "Just one more thing. I want an affidavit from both of you that O'Brien sent you out to kill me and referred to me as the Parole Killer when he did it. When the time comes to put the pressure on him, that will be one more piece of evidence. And it's also a good way to make sure two more crooks get out of town. You won't hang around O'Brien after this."

All argument was gone out of them. They signed.

"And now," Smith said, "tap them, Bushelmouth, so they'll sleep. I'll rent a car, ride the boys around awhile, then dump them where they won't be able to find this place again."

"Yossur."

Bushelmouth tapped them. They slept....

It was midnight, but lights still burned in the Vignaux home. Smith parked in front and went up the walk. There was a half moon overhead and in one of the magnolias a mockingbird was singing. Lightning-bugs hung their silver and gold lamps in the black tree-shadows.

Smith climbed the front steps and rang. A servant answered. "I'm sorry," Smith said. "I don't want to disturb Mrs. Vignaux, but I want to see Mr. Vignaux's study. The room where he was killed."

The negro butler hesitated.

Smith said, "I'm from headquarters, a detective," and pushed past him.

The room hadn't been disturbed except by the routine photography and fingerprint work. With the exception of the empty chair behind the desk, it was exactly as Smith had last seen it. He stood where he had stood before, his round blue eyes soaking in every detail. And as he stood there he was conscious of the pain in his cheek, a steady throbbing ache that covered the whole side of his head.

Smith had come here hoping to find some place to start afresh, some foothold from which he could once more attack the problem of locating Marion. Her kidnapping and this murder were connected. He knew that, and he knew that O'Brien was in on the kidnaping as he had been on the murder. But he had failed in his attempt at O'Brien, and now the politician would keep too many gunmen around for another try to succeed. Smith had to start at his problem from a different angle. But where?

"O'Brien probably came in here and didn't even take a chair," Smith thought. He began to act out the murder as he imagined it to have happened. And when he knelt beside the chair, pretending to roll Vignaux's sock as the murderer had done, he saw the handkerchief. It was far up under the desk and wouldn't be seen except by a person crouching close to the floor.

Smith pulled it out. The handkerchief was made of maroon-colored silk and in one corner were the letters POB worked into an elaborate monogram.

It was Pete O'Brien's handkerchief. Not the same one he had worn tonight, but evidently one of a set.

Had O'Brien dropped it there when he had killed Vignaux? It could have been dropped by a man kneeling close to the desk and kicked underneath. But why hadn't Smith seen it before? Why hadn't the police found it? He was willing to swear it hadn't been there when he examined Vignaux's body. Then when was it dropped? Why was it there?

HE WENT out in the living room, got the butler, and asked if he had a list of the persons who had called during the day. The butler said no, but almost everyone had left cards and he had them.

Smith looked them over. Most of the local politicians had come to pay their respects, but O'Brien hadn't. There was, however, one card that held Smith's attention. Dan Snyder. Boss Snyder. One of the state's most powerful politicians, but both he and O'Brien were too smart and too crooked to ever fight one another outright. So far Smith had been unable to connect Snyder with the parole racket. But if O'Brien wasn't the actual head of the racket, if there was a figure hidden back of him....

Smith asked if any of the callers had gone back into the room where Vignaux was killed and the butler said he didn't think so. Most of them had had the chance, however. Mr. Snyder? Maybe; he didn't know.

"Do you know Pete O'Brien, a little monkey-faced man?"

The butler said he knew him by sight. He was certain Mr. O'Brien hadn't called.

"Thanks," Smith said, and went back into the study. There was something damn strange here, and he couldn't figure it out.

He telephoned Rutgers. "I know who killed Vignaux," he said.

"Who?"

"O'Brien."

There was a long second's wait. He could hear Rutgers' heavy breathing. "Proof?" he said at last.

"I told you I was in the back room and heard someone walk out. I heard O'Brien walk tonight. He was the man in the hall."

Again the wait. "It won't hold up," Rutgers said. "A lawyer would laugh at that sort of evidence. We need something that a jury can look at and touch."

"How about a handkerchief?"

"A what?"

"A monogramed handkerchief under the desk. It's O'Brien's. It could have been dropped when he knelt to put the hypo in Vignaux's ankle."

"I don't know what you are talking about," Rutgers said after a moment.

"O'Brien's handkerchief. It's under Vignaux's desk."

"But it wasn't there," Rutgers said. "We would have found it."

"It's there now."

"A frame?" The words were very slow now.

"What do you care? O'Brien's guilty."

"You can't do it," Rutgers said. "I was afraid those damn ears of yours would make you try something like this—knowing a man's guilty and unable to prove it. But you can't do it, John. You promised me to keep inside the law."

For the third time that night Smith laughed at the word, a harsh terrible laughter that jangled into the phone. "Inside the law," he said. "Damn the law! They've got my girl, and I'm going to get her back. I don't care whether I use murder or arson or a frame—but I'm going to find Marion!"

Rutgers spoke quickly—"For God's sake, John, get some sense! You know I can't back you in this. I swore to uphold the law—and I'm going to do it."

"I didn't plant the damn thing," Smith said urgently. "If it's a frame somebody else is doing it. And you can't swear it's a frame. Use it." His voice got low again, grating. His hands were white on the phone. "I'm going to find Marion!"

He looked over the room once more but there was nothing else. He was leaving when the phone rang and he came back and answered it.

IT WAS Rutgers again. His voice sounded strained and unnatural. "A man has telephoned me, John, and insists that he get in touch with you. I'm plugging him through our switchboard so you can talk to him."

"And don't worry about trying to find me, Lieutenant," a hoarse voice said. "This is a dial phone and with the best of luck it would take hours to trace it." The voice was evidently disguised. There was a pause and it said, "Mr. Smith?"

"Yes."

"I'm the man who kidnaped Marion Dark."

Smith felt his body growing cold. The phone got very heavy in his hands. He was conscious of the pain in his cheek seeming to come from a long distance. He lowered himself into the chair where Claude Vignaux had been sitting when he was murdered.

"Are you listening?" the voice asked.

"Yes," Smith said.

"I've got a proposition to make. If you'll get in touch with me, come where I tell you—I'll tell you when the police are not listening, of course—I shall be glad to release the girl. If you don't, I'm afraid something will happen to her."

Smith did not answer for a moment. He couldn't.

This was the end, he thought. The whole thing was a plan to murder him. He would be walking into a well-planned trap. The end of his fight against the parole racket. Defeat. Deliberately breaking faith with the dead. The loss of all the two of them had fought for.

And if he didn't go? It would be sacrificing Marion Dark. It would be murdering the girl he loved.

"Are you agreeable?" the voice asked.

Smith was leaning against the desk. He felt very weary and a little sick with the pain in his face. There was no great struggle inside him; only a feeling of despair.

"Smith?" the voice asked.

"Yes?"

"Do you want the girl—or do you want to keep on with your fight?"

"The fight," Smith said. "It's more important than any one person, even Marion." His lips moved on the words, and yet there was no sound.

"What?" the voice said.

And then Smith heard words, muffled against the telephone's mouthpiece. "I'll do what you say. Where do you want me?"

"Good. Drive to the corner of Canal and Royal and park as close by as you can. Walk up Canal to the Terminal Station and back. I'll get in touch with you."

The voice stopped, then said, "And you, Lieutenant. You'd best let Mr. Smith do this alone. Any flatfeet following him, and the whole thing is off. It'll be tough on the girl."

Smith heard Rutgers sputtering and he cut in and said, "I'll be there—alone. But let me make one thing clear. The girl is going to be free before I step into any traps. If you try to crack down on me before then, you'd better be successful. One try like that and I'll know it's too late to help the girl. And if it is, God help you." He hung up.

He was very tired. His knees felt weak. The wound in his cheek was a dull throbbing ache that spread from temple to jaw. Vignaux had always kept a bottle of Scotch in the room and now Smith found it, took a jigger straight, then another. It was good liquor and Smith had always liked good liquor. There were a lot of things in life he liked. Well, he had to give them up someday. He tried not to think of the girl. It was a little bitter to know that in saving her, he was losing her forever.

He took the gun out of his holster and looked it over. There were fresh cartridges in his pocket and he made sure he could get at them easily. There might be a chance to strike one last and decisive blow at the parole racket. He'd at least go out fighting.

He took another drink of Vignaux's excellent Scotch. It helped the pain in his face. He went out of the study. In the living room the butler was waiting for him, but when he saw Smith's face he did not speak, though his mouth hung open and the whites of his eyes got large.

Smith crossed the lawn. The mockingbird was still singing and the lightning-bugs zig-zagged beneath the trees. Smith got in the car he'd rented, and headed toward Canal Street.

CHAPTER SIX
DEATH RIDES THE RIVER

HE PARKED a half block off Canal on Royal Street, walked back and started down Canal away from the river. It was the center of the city's business section, but now the stores were closed though lights burned in most of the windows; huge plate glass panels behind which wax models displayed the Fall fashions for women; a jewelry store where stones twinkled in the electric light and a clock pointing out that it was now one-forty-five.

He saw the whole city with that weird vividness his sight had possessed during the first days after his blindness: as if he were seeing it for the first time. Seeing it for the last time, now.

He reached the Terminal Station, waited several moments, then turned and started back. Occasional cars passed. Out of a side street came the sound of a woman laughing. Several couples passed, swaying slightly.

"We'll make it by the Silver Slipper and then...."

"I wouldn't go out with him, Tommy. You know that."

"Of all the lousy music...."

It was strange that these persons could pass him and not feel the shadow of death that kept so close at his side.

Nothing happened. He went up Royal Street and found the note in his car.

Drive to the Crescent Moon on Conti. I'll get word to you there.

The kidnaper was making sure that Smith wasn't followed. He could watch him arrive in a place, watch him leave. It was a good system. Smith drove to the Crescent Moon.

It was a dump. Poor light, an untuned piano banging, the odor of stale air, dirty tables, a bar. Smith went to the bar and ordered a drink, pouring it from a bottle that other customers were using. He wasn't taking unnecessary chances.

A girl with red hair and a white dress that was modeled to leave no doubt she was all feminine moved up beside him. "The liquor good?" she asked.

Smith said, "Foul. Have one."

She did.

A man with a scarred face came out from the kitchen and looked over the customers. He approached Smith and said there was a phone call for a guy named Smith who had a bandage on his cheek.

"That's me, I reckon," Smith said.

It was the voice again telling him to move on to a drugstore on Decatur.

He was starting out when the redhead got his arm and said, "What's the hurry, buddy? There's more in that bottle."

"You drink it," Smith said, and handed her a bill.

She looked at it and caught her breath and said, "What's this for? You want me to wait here for you? Hurry back!"

"It's because I won't need it any more," Smith said. "The odds are I won't be back."

From the drugstore he got directions to go to dock eighty-one. He knew the location vaguely and he had an idea this was going to be the end. "Listen," he said into the phone. "I want to know the girl is safe."

"I've got it figured for both of us," the voice said. "You'll see her turned loose before you see me."

There was nothing else to do; he wasn't in a position to argue terms. Smith went out Chantres, past the Navigation Canal, the Quarantine Station, turning back toward the river again on a narrow cobblestone street where arc lights were tiny pools of white in the darkness. When the street tilted up toward the river he parked his car and got out. It would be safer without the noise of the motor to confuse his ears.

AHEAD AND above he could see the dark bulk of warehouses that stretched to right and left. They had been deserted for years and from them came the odor that forgotten decayed buildings have, mingling with the smell and the sound of the river. A mosquito passed his ear, its whine loud on the empty quiet.

He climbed the levee to the wooden platform that ran for miles up and down the river on each side of the great sheds. Time and again he stopped, listening. He could hear the sound of rats within the sheds, the vicious whine of insects, the million-voiced river below him in the dark.

He turned downstream until he came to the end of this shed with a passage between it and the next one, and he crossed over to the river side of the platform. It was then he saw the boat tied up almost directly in front of him, a small row boat with a lantern on the empty seat.

The note was stuck underneath the lantern.

Paddle out into the river two hundred yards. I'll have the girl released on shore in such a way that you can see she is really free. I will contact you on the river.

He left the lantern on the dock and taking his place at the oars pulled out upon the Mississippi. The sluggish, heavy tug of the stream caught him. Green bananas floated by in the murky water, dropped from some ship unloading upstream. He heard the tap of bits of wood against the boat. He could feel the strength of the river, the mysterious hungry power that had swallowed into itself so many parts of life.

He was not accustomed to rowing, and though he headed straight out from the dock, the river took him down-stream. He saw, a quarter of a mile below him, the small glow of riding lights high above the water, and remembered that several abandoned freighters were tied up prow to stem and anchored well out from the shore-line.

Sound struck simultaneously at him from two directions: from downstream near the freighters and from the shore directly opposite. The low throaty moan of high speed motors. He looked, but there were no lights. The motors came nearer, the sound growing steadily toward a roar.

He saw the low dark hull of a speed boat a hundred yards away, saw it slice past him going up-stream, then swing and head back straight at him. At the same time the other boat closed in from below.

He knew then that he had been tricked. He knew, even before the lights lashed at him and the machine guns commenced their deadly stuttering, what was coming. In a rowboat, unarmed except for a revolver, he had no chance. The boat was frail and offered no protection. He couldn't reach shore before they cut him apart.

He knew it was coming and he didn't wait. He went over the side. Muddy water closed above his head.

Lights lashed out from the speedcraft, holding the rowboat in a brilliant circle like a picture flung upon a screen. Two machine guns went into roaring action.

Under water Smith heard the impact of bullets and the churning screws in that clear yet muffled way that water carries sound. His clothes hampered his swimming, but helped to hold him down. He tried to judge where the speedboats were from the noises, but it was impossible. The sound of the screws seemed to come from every direction at once.

He kept swimming. His lungs ached. They felt swollen, bursting at his ribs. His ears hurt and he could no longer hear the boats for the pounding of his heart. And when he could stand it no longer he struck downward with his arms and his head broke the surface.

The boats had criss-crossed, one of them up-stream and shoreward, swinging back again. The other was down-stream and toward the center but turning back. Its light was a white tunnel above his head.

He dived and when he came up this time both speedcraft were closing in again on the rowboat which was settling, the water within inches of the gunwale. He heard a man shout, "There ain't nobody in there! The rat got away!" The lights of both craft swung in slashing lines across the water. A third time Smith dived.

He knew there was no hope of reaching shore without being seen—even if he could swim that far with his clothes pulling at him and the blood beginning to ooze from his face again. The current was taking him down-stream and directly toward the abandoned freighters. He made for them.

WITH LUCK he reached them. They were anchored fore and aft, but he went past the forward chains and clutched at the one to stern. For a moment he merely hung there, panting. Vaguely he heard the siren of a police boat. The lights of the speedcraft were out now, their motors throttled to a whisper as they came down-stream.

Smith knew he couldn't stay in the water. His muscles were leaden and aching. The pain in his head had started again. He had to climb the anchor chain and get aboard the freighter. Somehow he did it, but when he legged over the rail he staggered, went down on hands and knees and then on his face. He lay there for a long while, pulling deep sobbing breaths through his open mouth.

He must have been unconscious for a few minutes because he never heard the boat come up to the freighter tied next to the one on which he lay. He aroused suddenly to see a dark blur of figures crawling the rail; then a speedboat swung out from under the stern and vanished downstream. Three men went forward into the dark rise of the midships deck, and disappeared.

Smith was on hands and knees now. He could feel his heart racing, but no longer because of exertion. He forgot the pain in his face, the water-tiredness of his muscles. He was thinking that he had first heard one of the speedboats coming from somewhere close by these freighters, and now....

The .38 was in its shoulder holster and he got it out, broke it, and dumped the cartridges into his hand. He tried to dry them and his gun, but he was too wet to do more than smear the water. He wondered if they would still fire.

On hands and knees he crossed the poopdeck where he had lain, eased down the ladder to the after welldeck. Here, if he crouched low, the solid bulwarks offered protection. Still waiting he crossed to the port side.

The ship on which he had seen the others was anchored prow downstream, its forward welldeck abutting the afterdeck where Smith crouched. He waited for a full minute, listening. There was no sound except the dim mutter of the river, the occasional creak of metal. He went over the bulwark and onto the deck of the other ship.

He crossed to the rise of the midships deck, paused, and heard the restless pacing of a man up somewhere ahead of him. A lookout probably. He'd take him first.

He went up the ladder to the midships deck without using the chain rail. Water made his shoes squeak slightly, and at the top of the ladder he stopped to take them off. Then he moved on again, soundlessly. He had the gun in his hand now.

It was easy. He waited until the man paced by, then let him have it over the head. He went down and Smith caught him so there'd be no sound. From the lookout's pocket he took a heavy automatic. He didn't like automatics, but he was afraid of his own gun now that it was wet.

There was the sound of voices now, very faint and seemingly miles away. Ordinary ears would never have heard them, and Smith couldn't be certain of the direction. He searched carefully through the cabins midship, but here the voices faded altogether and there was no living thing beside himself. He went aft again.

He didn't know much about ships and it took him several minutes to find the ladder leading down into the engine room. It was dark here, eerie dark and an environment with which Smith wasn't familiar; yet he made little sound. His left hand held the automatic; his right hand on the metal rail guided him. Socked feet felt carefully down the iron stair that spiraled perpendicularly down. He hadn't known the bowels of a ship were so far below the surface. His strained ears could hear the movement of the water against the ship's sides above his head, and from below the intermittent voices came clearer.

A pale spot of light showed before he reached the bottom. It lent a gray luminescence to the dark so that he could sense, more than actually see, the monstrous engines rising black around him. And then finally his feet were on the deck again and he turned forward toward the light and the voices.

The glow came from beyond a narrow iron doorway. He moved until he could see a table with a lantern on it. There were three men around the table, the yellow light striking shadows across their features. Two of the men Smith had never seen before, though he remembered them from pictures: paroled convicts. One of them was big and bulky and slow, whose crimes seldom surpassed housebreaking. The other was small, with long jumpy hands and a sharp face and eyes in which the luster was unnatural and the pupils contracted. A killer, a hophead.

The third man was Pete O'Brien.

AND BEYOND the table, tied to a chair, was Marion Dark! Her blonde hair caught the lamplight in flashes of gold and fire. Her face was deathly pale, but held erect. She was gagged with a strip of adhesive.

"All right," O'Brien was saying. "We can't afford to hold her any longer. We've got to get rid of her."

The hophead said, "Sure. Chief." His hands made a snaky movement under his coat and came out with a gun. "Now?"

O'Brien was afraid, but only his eyes showed it. "I—I wish that louse hadn't got away tonight. I'd feel better."

"Maybe he drowned," the big man said.

The hophead said again, "Now?" He was watching the girl, balancing the automatic carefully.

Saliva showed at the corner of O'Brien's mouth. "I… Yes. Now!"

"Sure," the hophead said. He raised the gun.

From the doorway Smith said, *"Not* now. Drop that gun."

The hophead didn't drop it. He had too much dope to think of anything but killing. He whirled and the gun in his hand blazed before he was half around.

Smith shot once, carefully. He wasn't accustomed to the .45 and he placed the bullet in the broadest part of the hop-head's body. It got him just over the heart. It slammed him back against his chair, and over.

Two things happened in the same instant. O'Brien screamed and went for his gun. The big man, blind with terror, dived straight at Smith.

O'Brien never got his gun out. The automatic blasted again and O'Brien crashed back to the floor. Then, head-on, the big man slammed into Smith. It flung him sideways. His shoulder and forehead slapped the iron door sill and he slid down it slowly to his hands and knees. He heard the big man storming up the ladder toward the upper deck, but his hands were weighted and he couldn't lift them.

Finally he was on his feet again, wobbling across the room toward Marion. His whole head ached and blood was running from the wound on his cheek. It took him a full minute to get out his pocket knife and cut the ropes which held her.

As she stood up they heard the crash of shots overhead.

SHE RIPPED the adhesive from her face with one fierce jerk. Her eyes were wild. "We've got to hide, get away!"

"Who is it?"

"The gold-plated squad! Lieutenant Shultz and his gangster cops. They've got orders to kill me—you—O'Brien!"

"O'Brien?"

But there wasn't time to argue. She was jerking at him, saying, "Hide!"

With one sweep he reached the light and extinguished it. The blind learn the feel of a room as quickly as normal men learn it by sight, and now Smith took Marion through the maze of engines to the ladder as swiftly as though daylight had flooded the place. They started up.

Above them was the sound of steps coming downward. The girl whispered frantically, "They'll meet us! They—" Then she felt him stop and move sideways and thought he had jumped the rail of the ladder and fallen.

"Here!" He was pulling on her, half lifting her over the rail. "Be careful. Now step."

"Where are we?"

"The top of an engine. I noticed it coming down."

They crouched there as heavy shoes clumped down the ladder past them. Flashlights flung white beams within inches of their heads. The sounds and lights went downward.

"Now," Smith said. "Quiet." And they were on the ladder going upward again.

There was nobody left in the police launch tied forward. Smith didn't know much about boats, but he managed to get this one started and get it ashore. This despite the girl staying so close to him that he couldn't pay strict attention to where he was going and could never use but one arm—except when he was using both on her.

"**SHE OVERHEARD** this man, whoever he is, this actual head of the parole racket, talking to Lieutenant Shultz. You've always known Shultz was a politician's baby and a crook. There are a few of them on the force, but they are hard to get off."

Rutgers' small dark face was vicious. He was one of these fanatically honest men who hate nothing except crookedness. "I think maybe we can get him off now," he said. "And those damn crooks he took with him. It makes me sick to think that thousands of honest cops have to suffer because now and then there's a crook. I'd like to have left the whole bunch on that boat until they rotted."

"Maybe Shultz doesn't know the identity of the man he took orders from," Smith said. "Marion overheard this telephone conversation before she was taken to the boat. She doesn't know where she was. She never saw the man, just heard him, and his voice was obviously disguised. Maybe that was for Shultz's benefit, if he doesn't know the man. But he knew enough to take orders. He was to bump off the kidnapers, including O'Brien, and to make it sure it looked as though they had killed Marion."

"But why did this guy want O'Brien killed? I thought O'Brien was the head man; and if he wasn't he must have been close to him."

"That was the reason," Smith said. "The pressure was getting too great on O'Brien. This man was afraid to have him around any longer. The real head of the racket figured that we would think O'Brien was the head. After he was out of the way, until the shouting was over and the public forgot, then turn up again. He must be the man who forced

O'Brien to kill Vignaux in person, then planted the handkerchief. He wanted us to center our fight on O'Brien, and forget everything after he was out of the way. I had an idea O'Brien wasn't the head man, but that he could tell us who the head man was. That's why I plugged him high up in the shoulder. But Shultz and his crooks ruined that by finishing O'Brien."

Marion Dark had watched them quietly. Now she said, "John may not know who the head man is. But he'll damn sure find out."

"Unless you are kidnaped again and he goes rushing after you and gets killed." Rutgers came as near to a smile as he ever did, thin lips twisted far back.

"They forced me to telephone him," Marion said. "I was supposed to say I wanted to see him. I didn't mean to, but hell! I was scared, and...."

"And then when you called you got your nerve back and shouted for me not to come over."

"Yes. They left one man there in case you did come, and the others took me away."

"And what are you going to do now?" Rutgers asked her.

She looked from him to Smith. She grinned.

"I reckon I'll have to look after her until the trouble's over," Smith said.

Bushelmouth came in with drinks. "You can cook enough for an extra person, can't you?" Smith asked.

"Yossur." After a moment he said, "You don't drink cawn likker, do you, Miss Marion?"

"Not if I can get Scotch," she said.

Bushelmouth retired, muttering.

"What's wrong with him?" Rutgers asked.

Smith said, "He's got to keep on buying his own whiskey."

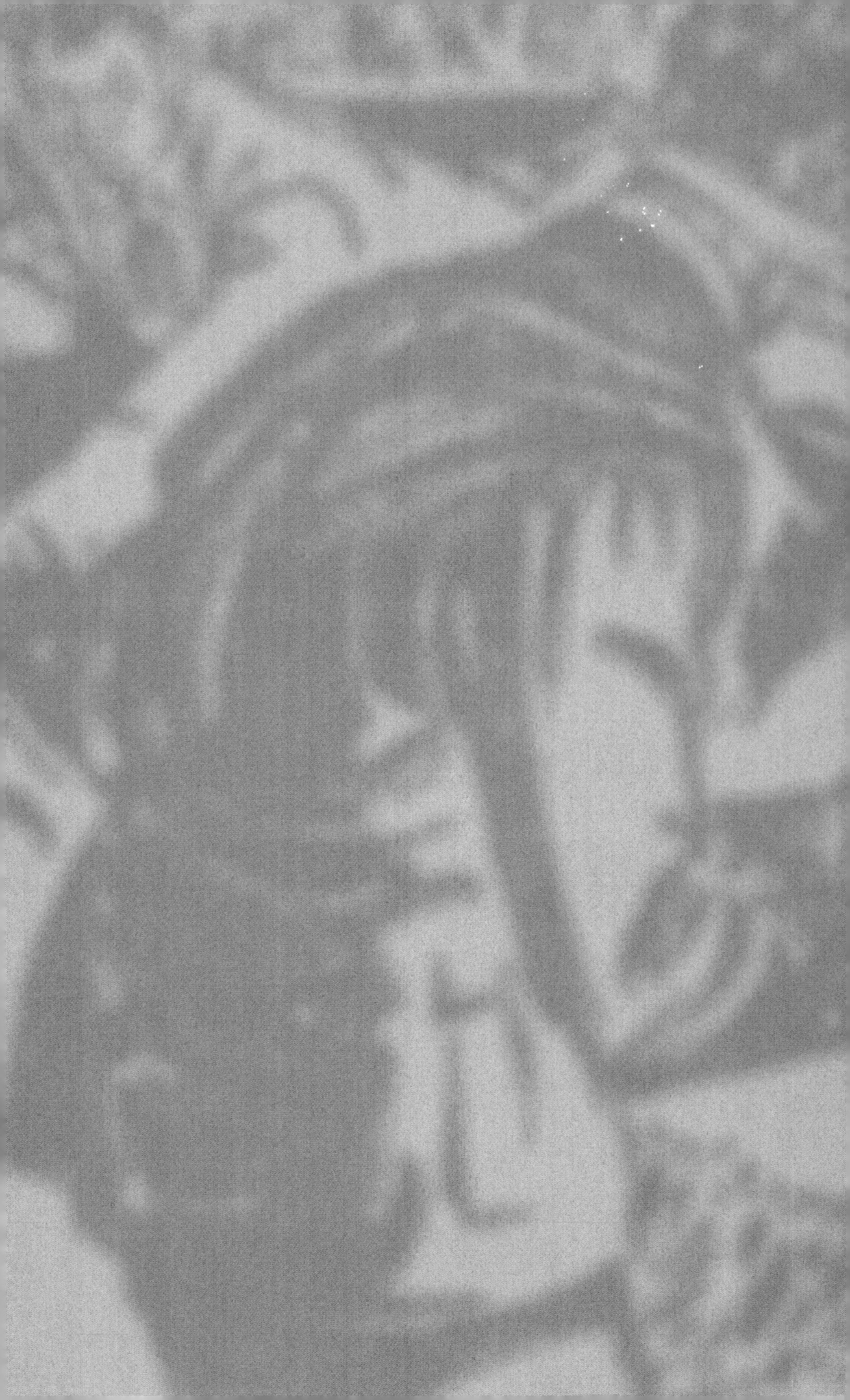

MURDER GIVES NO PAROLE

WAS THE PAROLE RACKET BROKEN AT LAST? WOULD THAT POWERFUL AND MYSTERIOUS FIGURE WHO STOOD FOR ALL THAT JOHN SMITH HATED, GIVE UP HIS CAREER OF CRIME SO EASILY? OR WOULD HE COME OUT INTO THE OPEN—TO BATTLE THE PAROLE KILLER UNTIL DEATH CALLED FOR ONE OF THEM?...

CHAPTER ONE
THREE FEATHERS
AND A PIECE OF HAIR

MARION DARK'S blonde hair was like a halo around her head and her eyes were such a deep blue they were almost black. She looked like a cross between one of Rafael's Cherubs and the Age Of Innocence.

She said, "Hell, you've got 'em licked. Monkeyface O'Brien's dead. There's an election coming up and the rats are heading for their holes."

"A rat never stays in his hole longer than he has to," Smith said.

"These will have to. If O'Brien didn't head the parole racket, he was certainly close to the head men. With O'Brien gone, whoever is the brains of the business will have to front for himself. He's too damn smart for that."

Smith stood up and crossed to the curtained window and stood there as though he could see through the window and the darkness outside and into some part of the future which other eyes could not reach.

"No," he said slowly, "I haven't won yet. Far from it. A racket as well established and as profitable as this parole racket, doesn't crack easily. I don't know who the head man is, but he and I have fought long enough to reach a sort of understanding. It's a fight to the death."

"John—" Her voice was suddenly fearful.

Smith did not turn. "O'Brien was sacrificed because I was getting too hot on his trail. But the other—the man who's furnished the brains—isn't whipped. He may be one of the boys who's yelling loudest for reform right now. He may not even be known as a politician. He may be anybody. The one thing I do know about him is that he'll keep fighting until one of us is dead."

"But can't…" She stood up quickly and he turned and saw how pale her face had become. Her lips were parted to say the words rising inside her, to protest at this ceaseless risking of life—and then she stopped, and forced herself to laugh with her eyes very bright and misty. She knew

Smith had his feet under him now....

that this job of crushing the parole racket meant more than life itself to John Smith; it meant decency, honesty in government, it was an obligation to those who had died in the fight.

"This is a hell of a place to ask me to stay," she said, smiling. "And you expecting to get it blown up or burned down any minute."

HE LOOKED at her seriously. "I've tried to keep this apartment secret," he said. "But it's certainly safer than letting you go around by yourself. They know you're messed up in this. They've tried to kill you before."

"All right," she said, still smiling. "We've got Bushelmouth to chaperone us, and if that doesn't work, well...."

"Well what?"

"Well there's been every kind of a gun but a shotgun mixed up in this already; though I don't know just who would carry the weapons and protect my honor."

"Maybe I could hold it against my own back." His eyes got serious again. A hollow feeling formed in his chest and the muscles of his throat worked. He said, "Marion...."

"Yes."

"Marion, I..." It was many long years since he had told a woman he loved her, since before that bullet glanced off his skull while he was still in college. He found it was hard to breathe, and his fingers were trembling. He turned sharply and called, "Bushelmouth, bring a couple of Scotch-and-sodas."

There was a wait and a voice from the kitchen said sleepily, "Yossur."

Smith looked at the girl again. He swallowed. Without facing the kitchen he yelled, "Make 'em double Scotch." And then, slowly, to the girl, "I think I'm going to need them."

"Both of them?"

"Maybe. Maybe you'll need both. Maybe...." He didn't say any more. He didn't know exactly how it happened, but all at once they were close with their arms around one another and their lips pressed close together.

Time acted in that strange way it occasionally does. It stopped completely and when it started again it had skipped several minutes. And during those minutes Smith's ears failed him for one of the very few times, since the long years of his blindness when he had had only his hearing to guide him and had trained it to almost superhuman keenness. He did not hear Bushelmouth open the kitchen door and then stop, gulping in amazement, a Scotch-and-soda in each hand.

Bushelmouth was very black and very huge. He had once been a leading contender for the heavyweight championship, but his brains had never been able to keep up with his hands and his feet. Now he acted with customary tact. He tiptoed ponderously across the room, put the drinks on the table, and tiptoed back to the door. Here he cleared his throat bashfully and murmured, "De drinks is on de table, Mistur Smiff."

Time caught Smith up with a lurch. He jumped and released Marion and gulped and got slightly pink in the face.

"Ah jes thought ah'd tell you," Bushelmouth said. He was backing out of the door and gestured feebly toward the table where he'd left the drinks, his gaze instinctively following his gesture. And then all at once there came into his eyes an expression of unbearable terror.

Smith said, "What the hell?" Then he, too, was looking at the table.

Coiling up from it was a little cloud of black smoke. As he watched, the cloud grew larger. In the still air of the room it overflowed the table, puffing slowly upward, growing like some monstrous mushroom. It began to swell outward toward the walls, to fill the room.

Smith's voice was like the crack of a gun. "Open that door, Bushelmouth! Open the kitchen windows!" He was moving as he spoke, whirling toward the curtained window behind him, thrusting Marion Dark to one side with his left hand as he let up the curtain, flipped open the window. He gulped a breath of air, keeping his head to one side, and leaped toward the light on the table. He was a small man but his movements had the oiled smoothness and rapidity of machinery. There was no waste motion in anything he did. He clicked the light out, whipped back and opened the room's other window. He pulled Marion down beside him, close to the window but sheltered by it.

The only light came greyly through the open kitchen door. And in the darkness they could hear Bushelmouth saying, "De three feathers! De gris-gris! De three feathers gris-gris!"

SMITH SAID, "Shut up, you fool. Shut up!" After that there was silence except for Bushelmouth's heavy breathing. There was a gun in Smith's left hand as though it had appeared there by magic. He was on his knees, the fingers of his right hand touching the floor lightly, head pushed forward and twisted a bit to one side. The muscles back of his ears strained until they ached.

In the silence Smith could hear the beating of his own heart, hear Bushelmouth's breathing. He could hear the footsteps of a man passing along the sidewalk outside his window. His ears, trained by years of practice, picked up the city's multitude of sounds. Radio-like he tuned them out one at a time. But there was nothing nearby, nothing furtive.

Ten minutes passed. The last faint odor of the smoke was gone, blown out by the wind. Smith stood up, closed and curtained the windows. He switched on the light.

"De three feather gris-gris," Bushelmouth moaned again. "Lawd, dey got us now."

"Look," Marion said. "That's what he means."

It lay on the table beside the light—three small black feathers tied together with a single hair and sprinkled with tiny pieces of glass.

For a moment Smith looked at it, then he turned and went quickly to the door. It was locked with bolts on the inside. He toured the rooms. They were on the second floor; there was no fire-escape and all the windows had locked screens. It was absolutely impossible that anyone could have got into this room. Yet the feathers lay there on the table where they had not been before. Bushelmouth had put the glasses there.

He looked at Marion. "How?" he said.

"I don't know. It—it gives me the creeps."

The phone rang.

For a moment Smith stood and listened to the phone without moving. He was thinking that, as far as he knew, only one living person besides these in the room, knew this phone number. That person was Lieutenant Paul Rutgers at police headquarters, and Rutgers would not call unless necessity forced him to.

Smith lifted the phone. "Hello," he said.

"So you've found my token," a voice said. "The feathers and the lock of hair."

It was a strange voice, very soft and slurred and yet more vibrant than any voice Smith had ever heard. It had a sort of hypnotic chanting sound.

Smith's jaw set hard and he spoke without parting his teeth. "Sure I found it. So what?"

"You don't know?"

"Voodoo maybe," Smith said with sarcasm. "You're putting a gris-gris on me, huh?"

"Perhaps it means nothing. It will mean nothing if you come to see me. I have information that you would like." The voice paused but the silence was pregnant with the echo of its chant. "About the man for whom you have been searching these months—the man who controls the parole racket!"

Muscles were cording in the back of Smith's hands as he held the phone. He had made a desperate attempt to keep his identity secret in his fight against the parole racket; the man whom the papers called "The Parole Killer," and who left his messages pinned to the bodies of parole violators had never been known to the public. But gradually certain persons had become convinced that he and John Smith, private detective, were the same. The underworld and the crooked politicians who fattened upon crime had sought for months the chance to murder him.

"Who are you?" Smith asked.

"My name is Father Simon."

"Where are you?"

"On South Rampart Street, more than two miles from you. But I knew the instant when the smoke coiled in your room and when you found the feathers and the hair."

CHAPTER TWO
THE MAN WITH THE SING-SONG VOICE

SMITH PUT through a call to Lieutenant Rutgers, said, "Have somebody watch that block of Rampart Street, Lieutenant. Get a radio car there within the next minute or two. No disturbance, just watch who comes and goes. It may be a trap, and if a few cops are hanging around, it should make a prospective killer hesitate anyway."

"They'll be there," Lieutenant Rutgers said. He added, "But be careful, John."

"That's what I'm doing," Smith said. He hung up.

Marion Dark was at the door, her hat and coat already on. Smith said, "You're staying here."

"That's what you think. You don't leave me in this place with things popping up in front of my eyes and nobody but Bushelmouth for protection. And I'm still a working newspaper woman."

"Ah ain't gwine be heah," Bushelmouth said. "I'se gwine see me a two-head doctor and git dis gris-gris took off, efen hit can be took."

"Come on," Marion said. She opened the door and they went out.

The house on Rampart Street was in a block of negro rooming houses, some of them fairly modern but rundown; others that had been built before the Civil War, magnificent old structures, long since gone to ruin, houses with classical lines of roof and arch, with rotting porches and columns broken and tilted, with filth over mahogany stairways, and with Italian handworked moldings breaking to fall and lie neglected in the dust.

A patrol car was parked in the shadows near one end of the block. Smith stopped beside it and said, "Which is the house?"

A man in the car said, "The third one on the right."

"Anybody come or go?"

"Not to that place."

"Thanks," Smith said. He drove to the third house on the right and parked.

"If he was here all the time," Marion said, "how could he have known when we found the feathers? And how did he put them there?"

"I don't know." Smith slid his left hand under his coat, made sure the gun was loose in its holster. He said, "I wish you'd stay out here, with those cops."

"Not a chance." She opened the car door and got out.

It was one of the anti-bellum houses. They went through a long empty corridor and came to a courtyard in the back. The place was littered with trash, tin cans, papers. A banana tree loomed black against the wall to the left.

There was a small house in the rear of the court, which had once been the quarters for household servants. A door opened and light spilled dimly out. A voice said, "This way, please." They went across the court and through the doorway into the smaller house.

The room was scrupulously clean but disorderly, piled with old odds and ends, furniture, bottles, bric-a-brac, so that it gave the appearance of being dirty. The only light came from black candles which ran along the far wall, and in front of these candles, his back to the light, was a man. He sat at a big desk which concealed most of his body, and his face was shadowed. "Come in," he said. He gestured to the two chairs pulled up before the desk.

Smith had stepped to one side of the door and put his back against the wall. For two full minutes he stood motionless, listening. But if there was any living creature in that room beside the three of them, it must have held its breath.

SMITH CLOSED the door and pulled a small table in front of it. With his right hand he took off his hat. He held one of the chairs for Marion, took the other.

"You are very cautious," Father Simon said. "In your position a man must be. But if I had wished to harm you I would have done it already."

"With poison smoke?" Smith asked.

"The smoke was completely harmless. I was simply exercising my taste for the theatrical."

"You took a lot of exercise," Marion said with a calmness she did not feel.

Smith's round blue eyes strained against the gloom which shrouded Father Simon's face. It was a thin, ascetic face without negroid features, though the skin was a deep saffron. The hands resting on the table were very long and slender.

"You wish to know why I asked you here?" he said.

"Right."

"One question first. Why is it you hate the parole system as you do?"

"Because," Smith said, and his voice took on a strange, hard quality now, "it is the foulest and most horrible racket ever inflicted on society. Did you know that practically every prominent criminal has done most of his work while free on parole? Dillinger, Floyd, Nash. Baby Face Nelson killed three G-men after getting his *third* parole. Read your daily paper and notice how time after time they mention crimes committed by some convict 'freed a week ago—or a month ago or a year ago—on parole.'"

"But why?"

"Politics. Crooked lawyers," Smith's voice was tight with fury. "In this state one man has controlled the whole racket, issued orders that politicians dared not disobey even when they didn't know the source of the order. When one disobeyed, something happened. Perhaps he was ruined politically. Perhaps he disappeared. Think of the power of a man who can charge criminals a fortune for their freedom so that they must murder and keep murdering to get money to pay him! Think of how the underworld will follow such a man! And all the while society suffers. Thieves and killers turned loose. Sex perverts freed to carry on their butcheries."

"No personal reason?" the man said. His gaze was on the pale scar that crossed Smith's forehead.

John Smith traced the scar with a slim finger. "Yes," he said, "there's a personal reason. More than ten years ago I happened on a bank robbery and was fool enough to interfere. A paroled convict shot me. The bullet didn't kill—it left me blind for ten years until an operation gave my sight back. Did you ever sit ten years in the dark, wondering if you would ever see again? Did you ever live for ten years with only your ears and hands to guide you? A young man with life running warm through you—and blind, helpless. Yes, I've got a personal reason to hate the parole system and the criminal who controls it."

"Those are your reasons," Father Simon said. "They don't concern me. But I can help you."

"How?"

"With facts."

Smith's right hand rested on the table, but his left hand toyed with the lapel of his coat, staying within inches of the gun underneath. His ears were strained, picking up every small sound that came into the candle-lighted room. He heard a rat scurry overhead, heard the ticking of a watch in Father Simon's pocket. Smith said, "What's your price? And what's—your idea?"

"**THAT DOES** not matter. Later I shall tell you why I am doing this."

"And suppose I refuse to pay?"

"You shall pay," the man said. There was supreme confidence in his curious chanting voice. And all at once John

Smith felt fear move like a cold feather along his spine. It was reasonless, eerie, the sort of thing that Negroes say you feel when a cat crosses the spot of your future grave.

"I have already taken care that you shall pay," Father Simon said. "But the price will not be too heavy."

Marion said, "Let's get out of here. This place gives me the creeps."

"You've already taken care that I'll pay?" Smith said. "What care?"

"I have put a small mark upon you, a small black mark to remind you of the black magic at which you laugh. When you pay—the mark shall disappear. And if you don't pay—"

"Phooey!" Smith said. "Is your help on a par with that?"

There was no change that Smith could see on Father Simon's shadowed face. The vibrant, sing-song voice said, "Three months ago parole was granted a criminal called One-eye Jones."

"One-eye," Smith said, "has been killed since then."

"Yes. But the board granted the parole because the board members got a signed letter recommending it—insisting on it!" Smith's right hand gripped tight on the table edge. The voice went on, "And one member still has that signed letter. His name is Thomas Wilkins. He has the letter in a wall safe in his office."

"You wouldn't know who signed the letter?"

"Boss Snyder."

"So!" Smith said. He knew Boss Snyder for a behind-the-scenes politician, a man who took no active part and yet was one of, if not the most powerful political figure in the state. Boss Snyder!

"How do you know about the letter?" Smith asked.

The man's lean hands gestured politely. "I have my way of learning things, many, many things."

"Perhaps too many," Smith said. He sat for a minute, letting his ears search the room and the darkness outside. Then he and Marion left as they had come.

They were half way across the court when Father Simon said after them, just loudly enough for Smith to hear, "I think you shall have one other man offering information. You will not trust him, but you will profit by pretending to." Then the voice died and they went down the long dusty corridor and out to Rampart street again.

There was a car parked outside Smith's apartment with one man in it. He got out when Smith and Marion stopped and came toward them. "Hello, hello," he said. "I've been waiting for you. Busy, busy as a bee these days, but not too busy to wait for John Smith. No sir." It was Carl Heikle, the man who had been O'Brien's personal and political secretary before Smith's gun had blasted the crooked ward leader out of this world.

CHAPTER THREE
THE CAT WITH THREE LEGS

MARION LOOKED at Smith and said, "What did you do, advertise this address in the paper?"

Smith said, "Let's go inside, Mr. Heikle. You first." But before Smith opened the door he crouched against it for a long minute, listening.

Carl Heikle was big and blond and stomachy. He took a chair where the table light barely reached his face and he rested his hands on his stomach and tilted back. He cleared his throat and looked at Marion Dark.

"Go ahead," Smith said. "Miss Dark is my, er, secretary."

"Oh yes, yes," Heikle said. "Well, I've come with a proposition, Mr. Smith. Yes sir, I think I can do us both some good."

Smith's face showed nothing but he was thinking suddenly of the last words Father Simon had spoken, hearing them as clearly as he had heard in that dark, trash-littered court: "You shall have one other man offering you information. You will not trust him, but you will profit by pretending to."

Heikle cleared his throat. "I think there is no longer any reason for us to pretend you are not the Parole Killer. That's become very evident, yessir, very evident."

"How did you find this apartment?" Smith asked.

"That's what I wanted to talk about. Now Mr. Smith, you know that I was Pete O'Brien's secretary and since his death, I'm in line to fill his place as leader of the 13th District. Yessir, I'm in line for the job."

"So?"

"Well, er, I—er—have the resources at hand that Mr. O'Brien had, and, er, one of Mr. O'Brien's men spotted you leaving here about a half hour ago. He telephoned me and I came right over."

"To make a proposition."

"Yessir, a proposition. There's no reason we shouldn't play ball together, Mr. Smith, no reason…." His voice trailed off. He was looking hard at Marion Dark.

Her face had drained white except for her makeup. Her gaze was on Smith, on a spot just above his right ear. Her mouth moved before she finally said, "John, I—I didn't know...."

"Know what?"

"You had that—black streak in your hair."

He felt the coldness around his heart before he understood her meaning. And then, as he stood up and went toward her, he was remembering Father Simon's words: "I have taken care that you shall pay. I have put a small mark upon you, a small Hack mark to remind you of the black magic at which you laugh."

He took the mirror from Marion's purse, leaned forward under the light. In the short-cropped blond hair above his ear there was a dark streak. And the skin underneath the hair was black also!

He rubbed it with his finger, licked the finger and rubbed it again. There was no change.

"What's the trouble?" Heikle asked. "What's gone wrong?"

"Nothing." It was only a trick, Smith told himself. Some trick that he didn't understand. But the cold spot was still at his heart when he said, "Go on with your proposition, Mr. Heikle."

Heikle cleared his throat. "There's an election coming up," he said.

"Yes."

"Well, er, there's been so much talk about politics and parole lately that people are all stirred up. I stand a chance of being turned out, my candidates may not be elected, because I was connected with Mr. O'Brien and the old system."

"Good," Smith said. He leaned forward in his chair. "You knew what O'Brien was doing. You're as crooked as he was. You should be thrown out."

Heikle got pink in the face and looked embarrassed. "Don't say that, Mr. Smith. I had nothing really to do with O'Brien's affairs."

"No?"

"Let's put it this way: I minded my own business and accepted politics for the way it's been played. There are dirty aides to every business, Mr. Smith. Yes-sir, I—er—I bet you get most of your information from stool pigeons. That's the way it is, a detective just can't work without 'em. And you accept them because that's part of the job. Well, that's the way I've played politics."

"And so?"

"I'm going to need your help in this election, Mr. Smith. You are the city's hero. If you were to say that I have helped you in the fight against the parole racket, I'd go in with bells on. Yessir, go in on a landslide."

"Well, I'll be damned!" Marion said. "What a nerve!"

SMITH LIT a cigarette. Through the smoke he said, "And can you think of any reason why should I tell the papers you've helped me?"

"Because I can. Yessir, I surely can."

"How?"

"I've got—" He stopped. There was a faint sound of singing from the stair and the thump of steps.

A soft voice singing:

"Now dot my ol' dog dead...."

"Who's that?" Heikle said quickly.

"Bushelmouth."

"De rabbits gwine eat my peas an' bread."

The door opened and Bushelmouth came in. "Howdy, Mistur Smiff. Don't worry 'bout dat gris-gris business. Ah got ol' Catgut Mamie to take hit off and when she taken 'em, dey stay took. I—" He saw Heikle and quit talking with his mouth still open.

"Thanks," Smith said.

Marion said, "Be careful, Bushelmouth. With your mouth open that way, an eagle is liable to fly in there and nest."

"Sho nuff?" Bushelmouth said. "Dere one loose roun' heah?"

"Go in the kitchen," Smith said. "Make some drinks."

"Yossur." He went, peering into the kitchen first to see if the eagle was there.

"And now?" Smith said. "That help?"

"Oh, yes." Heikle cleared his throat. "Mr. O'Brien kept some of the boys in line by the proper use of information he had. A little black book, but, yessir, he had the dope in it. I thought you'd like to have that book. And in return, well, I, er, we might play ball."

Smoke drifted slowly from Smith's mouth before he answered. "How do I know you wouldn't keep copies of the same information—to keep the boys in line?"

"It wouldn't be much good to me after you'd made it public."

Smith was remembering Father Simon's words that he wouldn't trust the man who offered help, but would profit by pretending to. That black book would be infinitely valuable, if he got his hands on it. Heikle was a crook, but Smith had an idea that even if Heikle went into office he (Smith) could keep the politician in line.

He said slowly, "It's a go."

Bushelmouth was coming into the room just as Heikle jumped up and grabbed Smith by the hand. "Fine! Fine! Now we are working together, you can smash the whole racket! Fine!" He took a drink from Bushelmouth. "Here's to it," he said.

Smith said, "Here's to it." He saw Marion's gaze on him, saw it shift to the black spat above his ear. There was something tense, almost frightened about her face.

Heikle knocked out the bowl of his pipe on the table and filled it. He seemed very pleased with everything. Watching him, Smith said, "Where is the little black book?"

"I didn't bring it, but I will. I—"

"You didn't trust me," Smith said. "Okay. That's mutual. And one other thing: *Who does head the parole racket?*"

"I don't know," Heikle said. "Maybe Mr. O'Brien knew. Yessir, maybe, but—"

Something beat at the curtained window.

Smith whirled, crouching and not breaking his movement until he had shoved Marion toward a sheltered corner and he was standing close against the wall near the window. The long barreled revolver was in his left hand.

There was a moment of utter silence. And then Smith heard movement just beyond the window, movement so soft and padded that normal ears would never have caught it. This was a second story window; there was no fire escape; yet something moved on that window sill.

With his right hand, gun ready in the other, Smith flung up the curtain and the window.

On the sill stood a black cat. The cat had only three legs. The front leg was missing and something was tied to the stump.

CHAPTER FOUR
THE STEPS IN THE DARK

WITH HIS right hand Smith brought the cat into the room. He lowered the window, pulled the curtain without ever showing himself. Then he took the cat to the table.

The thing tied to the stump of the cat's leg was cylindrical and wrapped in paper. Smith began to untie it, his eyes watching the movement of his fingers but his ears straining for a sound which he knew must come, although he did not know from which direction.

When he got the wrapping off the thing on the cat's leg he saw that it was a test-tube-like bottle and that removing the wrapper, had removed the stopper. Inside the bottle was a message written on paper, but the printing was so fine that he had to bring his head close to the bottle to read it. He started to lower his head. He did not know that death was escaping from that bottle mouth with a silence that only Death itself is capable of.

And then, overhead, he heard the movement: the whisper of cautious steps. He whirled from the table, got the door open and was in the hall running. A flight of stairs led upward to the roof and he went up them full tilt.

There was only a dull opaque reflection from the lights of the city and the indigo-blue sky in which a half moon was drifting downward. As he reached the roof he heard a sound to his right, spun, shoes skidding. From the top of the house next door a finger of flame leaped at him.

He fired, still skidding along the roof, and knew he had missed. Then he heard the clatter of shoes across the top of the other house. He did not try to locate the person with his eyes. For ten years he had practiced shooting at sound, for ten long years of blindness. Now he raised the gun, steadied it a moment, fired.

There were seconds in which all other sounds were lost in the boom of the gun. Then he heard steps hammering a tattoo upon a stairway, fading downward, and when he looked at the other roof he saw that a chimney stood in the direct line of fire. He said, "Damn!" and went after the man without much hope of catching him. He didn't.

When he came back to the apartment the cat was still on the table. But the cat was dead. Inside the bottle were the words:

When you have finished reading this it will be too late for you, and the cat, to understand that hydrocyanic acid is a gas and very very deadly.

Marian's face was bloodless, her voice husky with fear. "If you'd stooped down to read that, John... if you'd bent over that bottle instead of running up on the roof, you...."

"—would be like the cat," Smith said. "It's a good thing that stuff is so volatile that it has faded in the room."

Carl Heikle looked as though he had never been in physical danger before. He was backed as far from the table and the cat as possible and he looked a little sick. "What—what was on the roof?" he asked.

"Somebody. They lowered the cat to the window sill. Whoever it was must have been there when I came, or I would have heard his steps coming instead of going." He was looking straight at Heikle.

"My God!" Heikle said. "My God, Mr. Smith! You don't think I—I wouldn't turn loose poison gas in the room where I was!"

Smith's eyes were blue and very round and steady. "Maybe not," he said.

INTO THE telephone Smith said, "It may be a trap, Lieutenant, but it's too good a tip to turn down. I'm going out there."

"You don't put any faith in what that voodoo man said?" Rutgers asked.

Smith's fingers touched the strange black spot above his ear. "No-o," he said. "But I'm going to investigate."

"Then let me send a squad along with you."

"It won't work," Smith told him. "This man Wilkins, the parole board member, wouldn't want to turn over such a letter in front of witnesses. If he does want witnesses, I can call you."

"But suppose there isn't such a letter, just a plan to kill you?"

"I've thought of that. That's why I want you to have a few cops around the place. Tell 'em to come in if they hear any trouble."

"Okay," Rutgers said. And added, "Be careful, John."

Smith went alone, leaving Marion despite her protests. Lieutenant Rutgers had a couple of detectives watching the apartment now and it would be safer for Marion there.

Thomas Wilkins' house was a big, two-storied place on St. Charles. There was a wide lawn with the moonlight shut out by magnolia and water-oaks, a tall hedge that separated the lawn from the street. The house itself was dark.

Smith thumbed the bell and could hear it ringing softly far back in the house. Then he took his finger off the bell and the sound died and there was intense quiet. He waited a moment and rang again.

He heard steps now, though no light showed. They were careful steps like those of a man walking in the dark, but there was no attempt at silence. Once he heard the bang of an overturned chair and a man cursing. Then the steps came into the front room, crossed it, and the door opened. A man looked out.

Smith had seen pictures of Thomas Wilkins, but in the dark he couldn't be certain. He said, "Mr. Wilkins?"

"Yes."

"I wanted to talk to you. My name is John Smith."

Wilkins jerked nervously and Smith heard him swallow. He said, "Come in, Mr. Smith. I've blown a fuse and there are no lights except some candles in my study."

"Thank you," Smith said, and added in a conversational tone, "There are cops all around this place."

"What? What do you mean?"

"Maybe it doesn't mean anything," Smith said. "I'm just being careful." He stepped over the sill.

There was no warning. Thomas Wilkins pulled a blackjack from his pocket and swung at Smith's head.

Smith heard the swish of leather on cloth as the blackjack left Wilkins' pocket. He tried to dodge and pull his gun, but his foot slipped on the polished floor. Then the blow landed.

He did not go out completely, but when he tried to move there was no connection between his muscles and his brain. He felt himself pulled along the dark hallway and a door opened and he was in a lighted but tightly curtained room. His wrists were handcuffed together behind him and another pair of cuffs were put around his ankles. His jaws were pried apart, a handkerchief stuffed into his mouth and another tied around his face to hold the first one in place.

A voice said, "The girl didn't come with him."

"We've got to have her," a man said. "She'll blow the whole story apart."

"But how'll we get her? We can't leave here without being seen."

"Get her on the phone. That negro will probably answer, and he'll believe anything. Tell him to tell her that Mr. Smith wants her to come over with her notebook right away."

Smith's head was clearing now though pain still made things waver before his eyes. He cursed into his gag, fought until he was in a sitting position. Then a man's foot pushed him flat again. Somebody was talking to Bushelmouth over the phone. Smith tried to roll into the phone table and someone kicked him between the eyes. When his head cleared again it was too late to interfere.

He saw there were four men in the room beside himself. One of them lay on the floor, bound and gagged. He was a big whitehaired man with eyes that once had been icy and cruel but now they were glazed with fear. It was Boss Snyder. The other men were Carl Heikle, Thomas Wilkins, and Father Simon.

Heikle said, "She's on her way over Mr. Smith, yessir, on her way. You can understand why I've got to have her. Otherwise she'd blow up my gag about helping you with the parole fight, yessir, blow it wide open."

A desperate, heart-crushing bitterness filled John Smith. Month after month he had fought the parole racket, fought all its foulness and the criminals who worshipped it, fought against overwhelming odds in a desperate struggle to find the man who controlled it. Now he had found that man—when it was too late. And Marion also must suffer.

The thought drove him half-insane. Marion was coming here, thinking he had called, walking into a trap to be murdered in cold blood! A scream of desperation and fury came up in his throat and he had to fight to keep it down, fight to regain some measure of calmness. He had to think, find some way to warn her before she arrived!

CHAPTER FIVE
PAROLE'S END

SCRAPS OF information that he had picked up during the past months began to fit together in Smith's mind. He knew now that the man who had controlled the parole racket had not been Pete O'Brien or Snyder or any big-game politician. It had been Carl Heikle! He had posed as O'Brien's secretary, forcing the other man to front for him, finally having him murdered when the chase got too hot.

Smith had suspected tonight, but there had been no proof. When Father Simon had told him that a second man would offer him help and then Heikle had appeared, Smith had been almost certain there was some connection between the two. The cat had been lowered from the roof only after Heikle had made a rapping noise with his pipe on the table. But that was still no proof.

It was obvious now what Heikle had planned. He was afraid he would be voted out in the next election and a whole new set of officials would come in over whom he had no control. So he had planned to run as a friend and helper of John Smith—the head of the parole racket masquerading as assistant to the Parole Killer! And he had made elaborate plans.

Afraid that if he went straight to Smith with his story about the black book which O'Brien had used, Smith would throw him out, he had used Father Simon to build up in Smith's mind the idea that he would gain by pretending to agree with Heikle. And Heikle had made a big speech about them working together in front of Bushelmouth. The negro would believe it sincere. With both Smith and Marion out of the way, Bushelmouth would he Heikle's proof that he (Heikle) had been a friend of the Parole Killer!

Now Heikle stood beaming red-cheeked down at Smith. "I'm almost sorry it's over," he said. "Yessir, almost sorry. It's been a good fight, but I just had too much sense for you. Yessir."

"She must be nearly here now," Smith was thinking. "Five, ten minutes more and she'll be here." There were police outside waiting for a signal from him, but he was bound and gagged, with three armed men watching him. And Marion coming closer.

"To show you how I use my brains," Heikle said, "I'm making use of these cops you've got out there. Yessir, using them to prove how you and Mr. Snyder here—" he gestured toward the white-haired man on the floor—"killed each other. And killed the lady too. Charming lady, Miss Dark. Charming. Too bad she's got to die."

Smith growled into the gag and Heikle waved a chubby hand. "You see," he said, "we got here before the cops. Both the excellent Father Simon and myself lost those you had following us. A nice move that, to have us followed. Yessir, nice, but we lost them. Mr. Wilkins is supposed to be in Baton Rouge tonight. His house is supposed to be empty. And that's what the cops will think."

"She's only a few minutes away," Smith thought. "Coming here to die." His brain groped at a thousand wild schemes, and found nothing.

"You see," Heikle said, "there is a trapdoor in this floor that leads into a secret basement. Yessir, regular secret chamber like they have in picture shows and books. After you and Mr. Snyder and Miss Dark shoot one another, the cops will come rushing in. They'll find the house empty except for you three. The handcuffs and gags gone, of course. And in your hand will be the letter that Snyder wrote recommending the parole for One-Eye Jones. Even the police will figure that you both came here after the letter, and fought."

SO THAT was it, Smith thought. And the real murderers would stay hidden only a few feet away until the police were gone. Then they would walk free. Heikle would be reelected, a public hero, and would carry his men into office with him. He would talk louder about reform than anybody—for a few months until the public forgot. Then the old system would start again. Murderers, perverts, thieves, could buy their freedom with the loot of crime. The law would be a farce. The politicians would protect the criminals from the police!

And then his thoughts came back to the most horrible fear of all. Marion! She must be close now, perhaps just outside.

He got his feet under him as though working into a comfortable sitting position. As he moved he pushed his head hard against the wall, trying to loosen the gag. He knew it was hopeless to work on the cuffs. If he could only yell....

Heikle was saying, "I hate to get rid of Mr. Snyder too. He was a good man, yessir, pretty good in his time. But since I forced him to write that letter he's been too ready to talk."

Smith had his feet under him now. Headlong he dived at the table. If he could bring that down with a crash....

Father Simon's move was too quick. His body struck Smith's, knocked him sideways so that he banged into Snyder lying bound on the floor. Smith roiled on top of the man, his fingers behind him, groping. Then he touched Snyder's gag. He jerked at it at the same time that Wilkins' blackjack struck him on the forehead.

Wave after wave of darkness rolled over him. He fought for consciousness, seeming to struggle upward into dim light, then sink again. And finally he was conscious that Marion was there in the room. She was gagged, and Wilkins stood behind her holding her wrists.

Heikle had an automatic in his right hand, Smith's revolver in his left. "Well," he said, "the time has come. Yessir, it's here. You first, Mr. Snyder." He raised Smith's revolver.

There was a great stillness in the room then. Snyder's face was chalk-white with huge beads of sweat standing on his forehead. Muscles worked in his cheeks. Heikle's finger squeezed slowly on the trigger.

And then Smith heard the sound in the hallway. It was so soft that no one else there heard it, but Smith heard, and something flared in his heart—and his brain was like white fire. He tried to scream but there was only a muffled mutter. He raised his bound feet and brought them down on the floor with all his strength.

Heikle said, "Your turn next, Mr. Smith." His finger kept squeezing on the trigger.

The whole room exploded into action. The door behind Heikle banged open. The gig seemed to spurt from Snyder's mouth upon the top of one long, hideous scream. Heikle fired once, whirled, and fired again even before he saw the black giant charging through the doorway. There wasn't much of Bushelmouth's face to be seen anyway, because he was grinning and the grin covered everything except an unbelievable expanse of teeth.

He said. "Hot damn! Dev got guns!" Then as Heikle fired a third time. Bushelmouth hit him. It was a blow that must have started somewhere beyond the door and it had all of Bushelmouth's two hundred and thirty pounds behind it.

Wilkins had let go the girl and was spinning. A gun crashed in Father Simon's hand. And now the doorway was full of men, shooting.

When it stopped finally, there were four dead men in the room. Heikle's first shot had got Snyder. The cops had got Heikle and Father Simon and Wilkins.

"Lord!" one of the cops said, "that negro hit Heikle so hard that he was travelling across the room like a bird on the wing. When I shot, I had to lead him by two feet."

SMITH HUNG up the phone, read a page and a half in the little black book he held, then dialed another number. He said, "Hello, Mr. Hartwell? I've called to advise you not to run for the legislature. There's a little matter of some local paving contracts which I think make you unfitted.... Now just a minute, Mr. Hartwell. It's a matter of exactly $27,352.89 from July 1934. And there's that hunting trip over near New Iberia that might prove embarrassing. You remember, the one where you went without your wife? Now if Ruby was to turn up... That's good, Mr. Hartwell.

I'm glad to know you are retiring from the race." He hung up, read another page in the book and dialed again.

Later he looked at Marion and said, "I think that gets the worst over."

"It should," she said, "Bushelmouth knew it wasn't you telephoned from Wilkins. And I knew you wouldn't have given this number to anybody else. So I figured there must be trouble somewhere. I got the cops who were watching your apartment to come with me. We weren't certain, and Mr. Wilkins was too important a man for cops to come bursting into his house if there wasn't trouble, so they let me come in first. Wilkins did come to the door, and in the dark the cops couldn't see what happened."

"How'd Bushelmouth get here?" Before Marion could answer, Bushelmouth came from the kitchen with drinks. He said, "Ah tole you, Miss Mar'on, dat ole Catgut Mamie knew wha' she wuz talkin' 'bout."

"What?"

"He was worried about that three-legged cat," Marion said. "He called Catgut Mamie and she told him the cat had put a voodoo an all of us and we should take some of the conjure water she'd sold Bushelmouth. And when I said I thought you were in trouble, he came bringing the conjure water."

Smith said, "He gave Heikle a large dose of it."

"Dem policemens wouldn't let me hang 'round wid dem," Bushelmouth said. "Dey was jus squattin' out front anyhow. So I come roun' de back. Ol' Catgut Mamie says you was in trouble, so I knowed it wuz so."

Smith grinned. "Father Simon was an Italian pretending to be a Hindu. He used sleight of hand to put that dye in my hat and so stain my hair. And he used a simple trick with those feathers. He got in here, during the afternoon while we were out, stuck the feathers and a smoke bomb to the underside of the lamp shade with glue which took several hours to dry: When it finally dried the feathers and smoke bomb fell. Heikle or Wilkins must have been across the street and seen the smoke, phoned Simon. It was a neat trick, but it was the real voodoo that ruined them."

"Catgut Mamie de powerfullest two-head doctor in town," Bushelmouth said.

Smith said, "That was pretty potent stuff you carried in your fist."

"Yoss-ur." Bushelmouth thought a moment. "Dat gent'eman did have a gun in he hand, Mistur Smiff."

"So he did," Smith said. He got five dollars out of his pocket. "Get five times enough of that Bay St. Louis corn. Celebrate. And don't hurry back. I think Miss Dark and I have a few things to talk over that will take some time."

This is the last story of the Parole Killer Series. It seems a shame, though, to say good-bye to two such grand and courageous people as John Smith and Marion Dark. Perhaps the author has planned some more adventures for them—we hope so. We are going to ask him; and as soon as we find out, we will let you know.

Printed in Great Britain
by Amazon